I0581352

Savage Outcome

A Garrett Storm Novel

C. Marten-Zerf

Anglo American Press

LONDON, UNITED KINGDOM

Copyright © 2017 by **C. Marten-Zerf/Craig Zerf**

All rights reserved. No part of this publication may be reproduced, distributed or transmitted in any form or by any means, without prior written permission.

Anglo American Press
London
England
United Kingdom

Publisher's Note: This is a work of fiction. Names, characters, places, and incidents are a product of the author's imagination. Locales and public names are sometimes used for atmospheric purposes. Any resemblance to actual people, living or dead, or to businesses, companies, events, institutions, or locales is completely coincidental.

Book Layout © 2017 BookDesignTemplates.com

Savage Outcome/ C. Marten-Zerf/Craig Zerf. -- 1st ed.

Once again –

For my wife, Polly and my

son, Axel

Your light chases the

shadows from my soul.

Romans 13:4 - *For he is the minister of God to thee for good. But if thou do that which is evil, be afraid; for he beareth not the sword in vain: for he is the minister of God, a revenger to execute wrath upon him that doeth evil.*

This is a novel…that means I made it up, however…many of the people mentioned do actually exist. You all know who you are. Some of the scenes and places have been deliberately changed, this was done for two reasons, firstly to protect the identity of some involved and secondly as a narrative tool. If you would like to discuss the reality then please drop me an email at zuffs@sky.com

Flight SA107 touched down on the tarmac at Edinburgh airport at five fifteen AM.

The tall, muscular Zulu was amongst the first passengers to alight, leaving the business class cabin with no hand luggage and walking purposefully across the link and into the terminal building. He glanced out of the small windows and grimaced at the weather. It was still as dark as midnight and the driving sleet eddied and scurried around the yellow sodium spotlights like clouds of moths around a candle flame.

The people outside were bundled up in layers of clothing, heavy boots, jackets, scarves and gloves. The Zulu owned no gloves. Nor a scarf. He had never had a need for such clothing.

He wore faded jeans, hiking boots and a heavy plaid blanket shirt that he had purchased in deference to the subzero temperatures.

A bored passport officer flicked through the proffered green passport, checked his entry visa and stamped it. He looked as if he were about to fall asleep. No questions were asked. Not even the standard, 'business or pleasure'. The Zulu nodded his thanks and continued on to the luggage retrieval area.

He picked up his luggage at the carousel, a battered olive-green military issue rucksack. The fasteners had been padlocked with cheap but heavy cast iron locks and the carry straps had been replaced at some stage with two, wide hand-tooled leather straps. Various rents and tears in the canvas had been roughly stitched with thick Dacron twine. Patches had been cobbled over a row of punctures that looked suspiciously like bullet holes. Frankensteinian surgery. A resurrection of something that should have been long dead.

The backpack was almost as scarred as its owner.

He walked unchecked through the customs area, following the 'nothing-to-declare' route and past the arrival gates into the main terminal, scanning the waiting crowd as he did so.

The man that he was looking for stood out easily. Slightly over six feet tall, long black hair that curled down to his shoulders. Three- or four-day's growth of beard. Deep set eyes, as green as a lover's grave. A long length brown leather Barbour coat. Military issue boots. Jeans. Broad shoulders tapering down to narrow hips.

Although the terminal was thronging with people, there was a small area of calm about the man with the green eyes. As if a force shield kept all at least two or three feet away from him. A shark surrounded by sardines.

The Zulu walked up to the man with the green eyes.

'Garrett,' he said.

'Petrus,' responded the man.

They both burst out laughing and hugged each other roughly, banging each other on the back.

Garrett led the way to the car park and the two of them chatted away like a pair of schoolboys after a summer break. When they reached the Land Rover, Petrus threw his old rucksack onto the back seat and then they pulled off, stopping at the exit to pay.

Garrett drove down Glasgow Road heading for the M90, lights on and average speed down in the crowded traffic.

The heater blasted out hot air, fighting the frigid winter morning, warming the cab to an acceptable temperature. But when they hit the highway Petrus opened his window, allowing a tide of arctic air into the cab, dropping the temperature to below freezing in an instant.

'Hey,' complained Garrett.

Petrus took a deep breath. 'Sorry,' he said. 'I had to smell the land. I've been locked inside a tin can for a whole night and then straight into the car. I feel like I've been buried alive.' He dragged more of the cold air into his lungs and then sighed. 'That's better,' he said as he wound the window up and settled back into his seat again.

They drove on for another half an hour and then a gas station hove into view on the side of the freeway.

Garrett glanced at his gas tank and decided to pull in and fill up.

The two of them went into the kiosk to pay and, at the same time Garrett purchased two black coffees. Petrus went to the self-service counter and ladled six spoons of sugar into his cup before he took a sip.

'Gas is expensive here,' he noted as he watched Garrett hand over a wad of notes.

'More than double South Africa, but I suppose it's all relative,' said Garrett.

'Relative to what?'

Garrett shrugged. 'Actually, I don't know,' he admitted. 'But isn't that what everyone says?'

Petrus laughed and followed his friend back to the car. He glanced at his watch. 'Nine o'clock and the sun is just coming up.'

'Yep,' agreed Garrett. 'Enjoy it while you can. It goes down at half past three.'

'Will it get any warmer?'

Garrett shook his head. 'Colder, actually.'

Petrus sighed. 'Oh well,' he said. 'At least no one is shooting at us.'

They both burst out laughing.

The trip took a little under four hours and, by the time they cruised into the main gates of the laird's estate the sun was already low in the sky, squinting embarrassedly through the thick cloud cover.

Garrett turned off the sweeping driveway before he got to the main house and took a smaller narrow track for almost half a mile, eventually pulling up outside a thatched stone cottage.

'My house,' said Garrett.

Petrus grabbed his rucksack and followed Garrett into the cottage. It was a small, single room abode. A rudimentary kitchen area ran down the one wall, wood burning stove, a butler sink, running water a small refrigerator and a few cupboards.

On the opposite wall a large fireplace that had already been laid. Four small shuttered windows, a single bed, opposite was a new camp bed for Petrus.

Two old leather armchairs were situated on each side of a low teak coffee table. An outside bookcase on the one wall, packed with books as diverse as Shakespeare, beat author Jack Kerouac and the Garfield's Fat Cat three pack by Jim Davis. Petrus found Shakespeare to be obtuse and Kerouac pretentious. He liked the cat.

The Zulu approved. It was a man's dwelling, no fripperies or false finery. He threw his rucksack onto the camp bed and then started to undo the straps while Garrett put flame to the fire.

Petrus opened his pack and pulled out a few items. 'Here,' he said to Garrett. 'I brought you some cigars at duty free. Cuban.' He handed over a box of twenty-five Esplendidos.

Garrett grinned. 'Thanks,' he said. 'These are great.'

'Also, I brought this,' said Petrus. 'You forgot it when you last left.' He pulled out a large machete. It was sheathed in a shoulder holster that had been converted to accommodate the long blade. 'I also brought my assegai,' continued Petrus as he drew his lethal short spear from his pack. The eighteen-inch blade and short handle just fitted in the rucksack, packed in from corner to corner.

'Jesus,' said Garrett. 'How did you get this stuff through customs?'

Petrus shrugged. 'No one asked if I was carrying a spear and a machete, so I didn't tell them.'

'You were lucky.'

'Got anything to drink?' Asked Petrus.

'Loads, but I thought that we could go and meet the laird first.'

Petrus pulled a face. 'Tomorrow,' he said. 'Tonight, we smoke cigars, sit by the fire, drink brandy and talk. Tomorrow we do the whole meet and greet thing.'

Garrett smiled and nodded. 'Right. Tomorrow.'

They settled in beside the fire and talked deep into the night. Drinking cognac, smoking the Esplendidos and discussing past and future happenings. Communicating in half sentences and in jokes, as only close friends could. Teasing and insulting and complimenting in equal measures.

Eventually the fire burned low and they both crawled into their respective beds and found sleep.

CHAPTER TWO

Garrett touched Petrus on the shoulder and the Zulu came instantly awake, his right hand reaching for his assegai.

'It's me,' said Garrett. 'Time to rise and shine.' He thrust a mug of black coffee into Petrus' hands.

The Zulu took a noisy sip. 'What time is it?'

'Seven o'clock.'

'It's still pitch-black outside,' observed Petrus.

'Until almost ten o'clock,' said Garrett.

'What's for breakfast?'

'We'll be eating with the laird,' answered Garrett. 'So I'm not sure what we'll get but there will be lots.'

After Petrus had risen and performed the three S's, shit, shower and shave, the two of them climbed into the Land Rover and drove to the main house. As they approached, the huge gray stone edifice loomed out of the slowly gathering light. A building as stolid and ugly as it was imposing. A massive brooding testament to Edwardian era wealth.

Garrett pulled up to the back of the house and they entered via a side entrance.

'Servant's entrance,' quipped Petrus.

Garrett shook his head. 'No, the family use this entrance. The front door is simply too huge and it's far away from all the rooms that they use to live in. Kitchen, drawing rooms and so on. The front of the house is all entrance hall and ballroom and formal dining area.'

Petrus followed Garrett through a maze of corridors and into a large dining area. A twenty-seat table dominated the center of the room. High ceilings, large arched windows, deep pile maroon carpets and wood paneled walls. Along the one wall stood a heavy sideboard, on it an array of silver food cloches covered a variety of serving platters. Alongside them stood dewed glass jugs of freshly squeezed fruit juices as well as two tea pots and a Bunn flask of coffee.

Next to the buffet stood a man. A similar height to Garrett, gray messy collar length hair, an unlit pipe clenched between his teeth. He wore a kilt, white shirt and tweed jacket. Booted feet. Long faced with large ears and a prominent nose. He looked up at the two friends as they approached and his face lit up with a smile.

Garrett turned to Petrus and said. 'Petrus, may I introduce The Much Honored, Brody Macaslan, Laird of Braegorm.'

Petrus bowed deeply. 'I greet you, Inkosi,' he said, using the traditional Zulu word for Lord or Chief.

'Braegorm,' continued Garrett, addressing the laird correctly by his territorial designation, as opposed to his name. 'May I introduce to you, inkosana Dinangwe, known also as Petrus Sizwe Dlamini, eldest son of chief Dlamini of Drummond, the Valley of a Thousand Hills.'

The laird bowed back. 'Splendid,' he said as he shook Petrus' hand, struggling momentarily as the Zulu shook in the African way, reversing his grip half-way through and then changing back. 'Well now that's over with,' continued the laird. 'Please call me Brody,'

The Zulu smiled. 'Please call me Petrus,' he countered.

'Good,' said Brody as he clapped his hands together. 'Now, let's eat. The rest of the guests tend to sleep in so we may as well start without them, heaven knows when the blighters will actually deign to turn up.'

Petrus needed no encouragement as he grabbed a plate and started to lift the silver cloches and help himself to a variety of breakfast foods. Then, one hand holding a plate piled high with sausage, devilled kidney, bacon, gammon, fried eggs and black pudding, and the other carrying a mug of black coffee, he set himself down at the table.

Garrett followed with a more modest plateful of kedgeree and black pudding and a mug of black coffee.

The laird fixed himself a bowl of oat porridge with heaps of sugar and a large dash of Laphroaig whisky as opposed to milk.

As they started to eat a women entered the room. Small and pale, blonde hair cropped short, eyes outlined in thick coal, pink lips shiny with transparent gloss. She wore brown moleskin trousers, a cream linen blouse and ankle boots.

All three men stood up.

'My dear,' greeted the laird.

She nodded and then looked at Petrus.

The laird gestured towards the Zulu. 'This is Prince Petrus Dlamini,' he said. 'Petrus, this is my granddaughter, Alicia.'

'I've heard of you,' she said, her voice surprisingly low and breathy. Like a forty a day smoker.

'Good things, I hope,' grinned Petrus.

She shook her head. 'No.'

Petrus raised an eyebrow but said nothing in return, instead he simply sat down and continued attacking his mountain of fried protein.

Alicia helped herself to a cup of tea. Milk no sugar. She sat down at the far end of the table and stared out of the window while the men finished their food, then she lit a cigarette.

'Alicia, darling,' said the laird. 'Not at the breakfast table, please.'

Alicia stared at the laird for a while as she took another two puffs. And then she dropped the glowing butt into her tea. The laird winced as the water fizzed and a small swirl of smoke rose from the cup. Then he turned to Garrett.

'My boy,' he said. 'There will be four of us for the shoot. Myself, Sir Rupert, Colonel Ruttington and Wilfred Willbourne. They've all got their own rifles so no problems there.'

Garrett nodded. 'They do know that they will only be allowed to bag does, don't they?' Asked Garrett. 'Shooting season for trophy bucks is finished.'

'Told them,' affirmed the laird. 'The fellows simply want to get out in the open and take a few pot shots. Tell you what, let's go to the gun room and select a couple of rifles for you and Petrus. We can discuss the shoot on the way.'

'Garrett glanced at Petrus. 'You coming?' He asked.

'I'll take care of the prince,' said Alicia. 'Give him a tour of the old place, get him acclimatized.'

'Splendid,' exclaimed the laird as he left the room followed closely by Garrett.

Alicia lit another cigarette and stared at Petrus. The Zulu returned her gaze, calmly and without rancor and finally she dropped her eyes and stood up.

'Come on,' she said. 'Follow me; I'll give you the full guided tour.'

Petrus followed her as she left the dining room, casually flicking her ash onto the floor as she went.

'That's the breakfast or small dining room,' she said as they exited. 'The formal dining room is at the front of the house.' They meandered down a vast corridor and she pointed out rooms as they walked past. 'The top two floors are pretty much all bedrooms. I think about forty-six or so. Library, drawing room, study, second kitchen.'

The list seemed endless and as Petrus walked about the mansion, he noticed that, although some rooms were staggering in their display of opulence, others were literally falling apart with loose plaster on the walls and holes in the ceilings. An eclectic mix of prince and pauper.

'We have over four thousand acres of land with a loch and twenty-two miles of river frontage,' continued Alicia as she lit another cigarette from the smoldering butt of her last one. 'But I suppose that you're used to all this sort of shit,' she said. 'What is your dad, some sort of African king?'

Petrus shook his head. 'No. The king of the Zulus is King Goodwill Zwelithini kaBhekuzulu. My father is an Inkosi. A chief of the tribe.'

'But you are a prince?'

'Loosely speaking,' agreed Petrus. 'I am an inkosana. That translates to prince but it also means simply the eldest son of an Inkosi.'

'So do you live in a palace?'

Petrus smiled. 'My father has the second biggest house in the village. My mother, his first wife, has the biggest. My hut is no bigger than Garrett's cottage. Smaller actually.'

'But we have over sixty rooms here,' stated Alicia. She sounded disappointed.

'I can see that,' admitted Petrus. 'But you see, in Africa we have no need for such a multitude of rooms, many that simply sit and rot. We have not yet found a need for such rooms.' Petrus was vaguely amused by the massive stately home but he managed to keep his grin to a minimum.

Alicia glowered at the Zulu.

'I'm going back to my rooms,' she said to Petrus. 'I'm sure that you can show yourself out.'

Petrus nodded his goodbye as he watched her leave.

As she turned the corner at the end of the corridor, she heard his deep chuckle reverberate through the hallway and she walked faster to escape the sound.

ir Rupert carried a Westley Richards .375 H&H rifle. He stood six feet five inches tall and probably weighed as much as a medium size fourteen-year-old boy. Garrett had met him before and found him to be a genuinely nice person, albeit a clichéd caricature of the quintessential English upperclass twit. No chin, large nose and ears and bad teeth.

The colonel had a Banser .300 WSM, a good allpurpose rifle that was well kept and well used.

However, one look at the colonel's eye glasses and it was obvious that shooting with him would most probably involve more luck than skill. Garrett had never seen such thick lenses before. They were the proverbial bottom-of-a-coke-bottle.

And to compound his terrible sight the colonel appeared to be almost totally deaf as well, causing him to bark his sentences at top volume whenever he spoke.

Wilfred Willbourne was the third guest and he sported a hand finished Holland & Holland 30-06 rifle with a Mauser action. A hunting rifle that most likely cost more than the average family home in the United Kingdom.

He was a short man who attempted to stand tall, his flabby stomach bulging over his too-tight trousers and his chest filled his shirt as taut as a sausage-skin. Jaw aggressively thrust forward, slightly knock-kneed and a doughy face with bright red cheeks.

He looked at both Garrett and Petrus with distain and, when introduced, deigned to shake Garrett's proffered hand.

Petrus had declined a rifle, claiming that he couldn't be bothered to carry a weapon on his holidays.

They used the Land Rover to get past the loch and into the interior of the estate, amongst the foothills of the surrounding mountains. An area that literally teemed with both Roe and Red deer.

When they all climbed out of the car, the colonel beckoned to Garrett. 'I say, chap, I wonder if your Askari could carry my rifle?' He bellowed, pointing at Petrus. 'Got a touch of arthritis in the shoulder and it's playing up a bit.'

Garrett's face immediately assumed a thunderous expression, but before he could say anything Petrus ran over, came to attention in front of the colonel and saluted.

'Me be honored to carry your rifle, Bwana,' he said with a wide grin. 'Me take top care of it, Bwana colonel sir.'

The colonel handed his rifle over and Petrus saluted again and slung the strap over his shoulder.

'You're not funny, you know,' whispered Garrett to his friend.

'I had to do something, before you lashed out at the old bugger.'

'He's a racist prick,' continued Garrett.

Petrus shook his head. 'No, he's not. He's just old and ignorant.'

Willbourne strode over to Petrus and held out his rifle. 'There you go, chap,' he said. 'Might as well carry mine as well while you're about it.'

Petrus stared at the pudgy man and then shook his head. 'In your dreams, boy.'

Willbourne glared at the Zulu but Petrus simply ignored him.

Garrett set off along a trail, checking for spoor as he did so and the rest of the men followed him with Petrus bringing up the rear.

After half an hour or so Garrett held up his hand, clenching his fist in a signal to halt. Then he beckoned to the laird who walked up next to him.

Garrett pointed across the valley. 'There,' he said in a low voice. 'A stag and three hinds. We need to work our way to the right, over by the stone cairn. Should be able to get a good shot then.'

Willbourne stomped over and peered at the small herd. 'I think that I'll take a pot shot from here,' he announced as he unslung his rifle.

Garrett shook his head. 'No. We need to get closer.'

'Bullshit,' stated Willbourne. 'If we try to get any closer, we'll scare them off. I reckon that I should take a shot.'

Petrus walked over and looked at the deer. 'It's easy to get closer,' he said.

'Rubbish,' responded Willbourne. 'Just because you live in the bush doesn't make you an authority on deer hunting, good fellow.'

Petrus raised an eyebrow but said nothing.

Garrett started to talk to the laird but his sentence was cut off as Willbourne raised his rifle to his shoulder and fired.

The shot went wide and the herd scattered and ran.

'I told you not to shoot,' said Garrett through gritted teeth.

'So what,' said Willbourne. 'I don't have to listen to the hired help.'

'Really, Wilfred,' interjected the laird. 'Why don't you come off it, old chap? You really are acting like the worst sort.'

Willbourne looked suitably chastised but that didn't stop him mumbling under his breath. 'I'll take the shot when I want to, bloody hell.'

Garrett composed himself and led the party down a different track, once again casting for fresh spoor. Forty minutes later he pointed out another small herd. Two hinds and a stag.

'So, you reckon that you can get closer?' sneered Willbourne at Petrus.

The Zulu stared at the podgy man for a few seconds then he simply stood up and handed the colonel's rifle to Garrett, taking off his blanket shirt as he did. Underneath, he had on his shoulder rig, containing his assegai.

His bare torso rippled with muscle and the weak winter sun threw his countless scars into stark relief. Long ragged slash wounds, short indented stab wounds and a row of puckered holes that were obviously bullet scars.

He drew his blade with a steel rasp and Willbourne took a step back, his face drained of all color as his eyes fixated on the two feet of razor-sharp steel.

Without a word, Petrus turned and ran into the heather and the gorse, his steps long and loping. Smooth as a thoroughbred race horse.

Within seconds he had simply disappeared. Vanishing into the landscape like he was part of it.

'What the fuck?' stammered Willbourne.

The colonel gave a chuckle. 'Seen this sort of thing before,' he said. 'Maasai warriors. Saw one kill a lion with a spear once. Bloody impressive, don't you know?'

He walked over to Willbourne, leaning in close as he spoke. As if he was sharing an intimate secret. 'Word of advice, Wilf, old chap. I'd watch my mouth if I were you. Chances are, if you keep offending the Askari, he'll gut you like a fish.

'I remember the Mau Mau in Kenya, 1953, night of the long knives. I was stationed there with The Black Watch, bloody locals went on a rampage, gutted a whole bunch of unsuspecting colonials. We had to discipline them of course, ending up killing over five thousand of the buggers.

'Great weather though, always sunny, don't you know?'

He chuckled to himself and took out a pipe that he clenched between his teeth without lighting. 'Gut you like a fish,' he repeated.

Willbourne delved into his shooting jacket and drew out a silver flask that he uncapped and took a swig from. The smell of single malt whisky wafted through the group.

Garrett kept his eyes on the herd of deer, trying to spot Petrus as he stalked them even though he knew it to be a waste of time and effort. If his friend did not want to be seen then he simply would not be seen.

There was a flurry of movement and the small herd scattered and disappeared over the crest of the hill.

'Ha,' declared Willbourne. 'So much for that. Scared them away, just as I said.'

But Garrett said nothing because he had been watching much closer than the others so he was the only one to notice that, out of the herd of three animals, only two ran over the hill.

'Come along then,' said Willbourne with a smirk on his face. 'Farce is over, let's continue.'

Garrett raised his hand. 'Just a moment, mister Willbourne,' he said. 'Let's wait for Petrus.'

'Why?'

'Because he's part of the group,' snapped the laird. 'That's why, Willbourne.'

Once again, the podgy man looked a little sheepish and, once again, he muttered a comeback under his breath. 'Don't see why we have to wait for him. Bloody cheeky sod that he is.'

So, the men waited.

The colonel chewed on the stem of his pipe.

Willbourne drank from his flask, without offering, and mumbled to himself as he did so.

And Garrett and the laird stood patiently and scouted the landscape.

Suddenly and without warning Petrus appeared out of the long grass, like a wraith rising from a grave. Over his shoulders he carried a two-hundred-pound hind. Its throat had been cut and the blood had run down Petrus' shoulders and onto his chest.

He dropped the carcass down at Willbourne's feet and then he raised his assegai above his head and shouted.

'*Ngadla*! I have eaten!' Then he leant towards the podgy man and said in a voice as low as a lover's whisper and as clear as thunder. 'You see, it is possible to get closer.' Willbourne shrank back. 'And the next time that you speak to me,' continued Petrus. 'You will address me as inkosana Dinangwe, or prince

Dinangwe. Not boy, or fellow, or chap. Do you understand?'

Willbourne nodded, his movements jerky and uncoordinated as fear stole his ability to perform simple motor skills.

'Good,' said Petrus as he stole a sly sideways glance at the colonel. 'Because if you forget, I may have to gut you like a fish.'

The colonel burst out laughing.

CHAPTER FOUR

Garrett was driving the Land Rover along the track that led to his cottage. Petrus and he had decided to spend an evening at the local pub after the disastrous shooting day.

The shoot had ended rather abruptly after Petrus had dumped the deer carcass at Willbourne's feet and then threatened him with disembowelment. And, although the colonel had found the whole thing hugely amusing, the laird was less than pleased with all involved.

The party had returned to the manor house in an uncomfortable silence, and Willbourne had returned to London early as he complained of a sudden illness.

The colonel and sir Rupert had stayed on and Garrett and Petrus had returned to Garrett's cottage.

And now the two of them were off to the pub to sit next to the fire, have a meal and sink a few beers.

As the Land Rover approached the main driveway, Garrett's cell phone rang. He took it from his shirt pocket and answered. 'Yes?'

'Garrett, it's Alicia. I saw your lights coming down the track. Are you and Petrus going out?'

'Yes,' affirmed Garrett.

'Where?'

'The pub. Quiet drink. Very boring.'

'Fine,' said Alicia. 'Pick me up at the side door. I'll come along.'

Garrett disconnected and swore under his breath.

'What's the problem?' Asked Petrus.

'That bloody spoiled brat, Alicia. She wants us to pick her up so that she can come with us to the pub.'

Petrus shrugged. 'Ignore her.'

Garrett shook his head. 'Can't do that. It would upset the laird.'

'Well then, pick her up. It's no hassle.'

'Trust me, my friend. She's always a hassle,' grunted Garrett as he turned towards the manor house.

He pulled up outside the side door and Alicia was already there. She wore jeans, black ankle boots, a black grandpa shirt, probably silk, and a large Barbour tweed jacket for warmth. Her face was made up in her customary fashion, dark lined eyes and shiny lips.

Petrus stepped out of the Land Rover and opened the back door for her. She climbed in without thanking him and they set off.

It was a short drive to the local watering hole and Garrett parked outside and led them in. A typical Highland Pub. Large inglenook fireplace blazing high on the one side of the room. A bar ran down the opposite wall and a selection of tables were scattered around the rest of the room. Some of the tables were set for diners and others were left unlaid for people that simply wanted to drink.

The walls were wood paneled in dark oak and the exposed beams were covered in sprigs of heather and dried thistles.

Garrett chose a table laid for dining and sat Alicia and Petrus down.

'Drink?' he asked.

Petrus nodded. 'For sure. Whatever you're having.'

'Drambuie for me,' instructed Alicia.

Garrett went to the bar and waited in the short queue.

While he was away from the table, Alicia spoke to Petrus.

'So have you been friends with him for long?' she asked.

Petrus nodded. 'A lifetime in deeds. Perhaps not so long timewise. He is a good man. Saved my life.'

'Oh yes,' agreed Alicia. 'He's a bloody hero. Saved my life too. I suppose he told you?'

Petrus shook his head.

'Well allow me,' continued Alicia. 'He burst into my life uninvited, and saved me from a life of drugs and degradation,' she said sarcastically. 'Then he simply beat up all of my friends and forced me to come home.'

'Yes,' agreed Petrus. 'He is a good man. A kind man.'

Alicia snorted. 'I'm being facetious. I mean really. Would you have done what he did? Simply barge in and beat up my friends just because they disagreed with you and tried to stop him taking me?'

Petrus shook his head. 'No.'

'Well, there,' retorted Alicia smugly.

Petrus turned to look at her and his dark eyes tore into her soul.

'I would have killed them all,' he said. 'But Garrett, he is a kind man. Soft in many ways. You are lucky to have him as your protector. He would die for you without asking even a question.'

Alicia looked shocked and her eyes glazed over briefly with unshed tears. And then she turned away from Petrus. 'He's just a game warden. My grandfather's lackey.'

'Yes,' agreed Petrus. 'In your eyes he will remain whatever you decide to see.'

Garrett returned with a small glass of Drambuie whisky liqueur, and two tankards of McEwan's Scotch Ale.

Petrus took a tentative sip and then nodded in approval.

'Now that tastes like more,' he said appreciatively.

Alicia sipped at her liqueur, eyes downcast, while both Garrett and Petrus applied their full attention to their beers.

At that moment a group of men barreled into the pub, pushing in through the front door, singing as they entered.

> *O flower of Scotland*
> *When will we see your like again*
> *That fought and died for*
> *Your wee bit hill and glen*

One of the men, a giant who stood over six feet five and was as wide as two normal men, leered at Alicia and blew her a kiss.

'Oh, fuck off,' she said.

'Hey,' the man responded. 'Watch your mouth, you silly cow. I was just flirting, no harm meant.'

Alicia stuck her finger up at him and the rest of the men laughed and jeered, but the recipient was less than amused.

'Fuck you bitch,' he growled. 'I was just having a bit of fun you ugly fuck.'

Alicia turned to Garrett. 'Well, aren't you going to do something?'

He shook his head. 'No.'

'They're insulting me.'

'They don't mean anything by it,' said Garrett. 'They're drunk, and you have no social skills. Just ignore them and it'll blow over.'

Alicia knocked back the rest of her drink, then stood up and deliberately walked over to the crowd of men who were now standing at the bar and distributing beers amongst themselves.

The men saw her coming and one of them laughed. 'Ooh, Macalister,' he said to the big man. 'You're in big trouble now; the lassie's coming to serve up some discipline.'

'Fuck her,' he boomed. 'Cow has no sense of humor.'

Alicia walked up to the bar, grabbed a tankard of beer and upended it on the giant's chest.

'You bitch,' he roared. 'Enough is enough, now I'm going to slap some manners into you.'

Garrett sighed and stood up.

He walked over to the fracas and held his hand up. 'Sir,' he said. 'I must apologize for my companion's behavior. Please allow me to buy you and your friends a round of drinks on me.'

'He insulted me,' shrieked Alicia. 'And he said that he was going to hit me.'

'Jesus Christ,' cursed Garrett. 'Why are you doing this? Just go back to the table, sit down and shut up.'

Petrus walked over and guided Alicia back to their table. Then he returned and pulled a wad of notes from his pocket. 'Come on, guys,' he said. 'Let's get some drinks in with our apologies.'

The huge man jabbed Petrus in the chest with his frankfurter-sized forefinger. 'I don't want your money, boy,' he said. 'So, fuck off back to your table before I'm forced to knock you about a bit.'

Petrus reacted instantly, grasping the man's finger and punching it backwards. The crack of it snapping was easily audible above the general background noise. Then the Zulu twisted and pushed the giant to his knees.

'Who's your boy?' he demanded.

Another man from the group lunged towards Petrus but the Zulu warrior simply backhanded him with his left hand, snapping his head back and sending him somersaulting over a table. Then he grabbed a steak knife off the table next to him and laid it on the giant's cheek, the point resting millimeters from his eye.

'No, Petrus,' shouted Garrett. 'Not here. We don't do that here.'

Another man jumped forward and Garrett clothes-lined him with a straight arm to the neck. The man fell to the floor, choking and clutching his throat.

The pub fell completely silent, apart from the sound of the giant, whimpering and mewling.

Petrus bent forward, brought his face close and talked in a harsh whisper.

'My friend doesn't want me to kill you,' he said as he cocked his head to one side. 'You see, he is a soft man. A gentle man. A nice man. But I am not a nice man,' Petrus continued as he put a little more pressure on the steak knife.

In the background, Alicia smiled smugly.

'But I am a guest here,' explained Petrus. 'So, for today, you live.' He slapped the giant across his face, driving him to the floor.

And then he flicked the steak knife under hand, throwing it at the pub dartboard in the corner of the room.

It pegged deep into the center of the board with a loud thud.

'Come on,' he said as he stood up. 'Let's go.'

The three of them left the silent pub and walked to the Land Rover.

Garrett opened the driver's door and climbed in.

But before Alicia could get in Petrus grabbed her arm.

'You play a dangerous game, child,' he said.

'I don't know what you're talking about.'

'Yes, you do. You seek to prove that he will protect you, no matter what. Well, he will, but be aware. You poke a stick at the Beast, attempting to waken it and one day you will. And you do not want that to happen, ever. Believe me when I say that. There will be no turning back from what might happen. You will have opened the box and unleashed the storm. And you cannot put a storm back into a box – it cannot be done. Now get in the car.'

The laird stood and looked out of the window but it was obvious to Garrett that, although he was looking, he was not seeing, he was simply facing that way while he thought.

'So, my boy,' he said. 'Heard that there was a bit of a to do in the pub last night.'

Garrett shrugged. 'No big deal,' he said. 'No one hurt. Well, not badly.'

'All's well that ends well and so on,' mumbled the laird. 'However, I was wondering if perhaps you could do me a favor, my boy.'

'Anything,' responded Garrett.

'It's nothing serious. Actually, only wanted you to do a bit of a survey of my holdings up North. You know, the estate past Inverness. I need the place given the once over. There are a few ancient crofters' cottages and such what, on the land. If you could take a look at them, get a general feel of their condition and then report back. Also do a bit of a game count, check out the stocks and general condition. That would be greatly appreciated, my boy. You could take Petrus along, I'm sure that he would enjoy it as well as finding it most informative.'

Garrett smiled to himself. The laird was being as diplomatic as possible.

'I think that's a great idea, Brody,' he said. 'Plus, it has the added advantage of getting Petrus out of the general populous so that he can do less harm.'

'No, no,' argued the laird. 'That wasn't my intention at all.'

'Well, it would be mine,' laughed Garrett.

The laird chuckled. 'I must admit, he is rather a rambunctious fellow, isn't he? Very primal. A force of nature, as it were.'

'And he's doing his level best to be calm and unobtrusive,' added Garrett. 'You should see him when he's setting out to disrupt.'

'Rather not,' urged the laird. 'Not if that's in any way avoidable.'

'I'll set off this morning,' said Garrett. 'And you're right; I think that Petrus will enjoy himself. At very least the weather and the terrain should prove interesting, especially as we'll be sleeping outdoors.'

The two men shook hands and Garrett left the laird's study, closing the door behind him.

He walked down to the breakfast hall where Petrus was eating alone, shoveling food from a plate full of his usual choice of mountains of fried protein. Bacon, lamb chops, sausages and black pudding.

'Hey,' he greeted Petrus.

'Hey,' mumbled the Zulu.

'The laird wants a favor from us.'

'No problem,' said Petrus. 'Who do we have to kill?'

Garrett laughed even though he knew that Petrus was only half joking. 'No, nothing like that. He wants us to check out his upper Highland estate. It's further north. Needs the game surveyed, buildings checked out, whatever.'

'We're being banished?' asked Petrus.

'He says no.'

'He lies,' said Petrus without rancor. 'But that sounds like it could be interesting. When do we go?'

'Might as well leave ASAP,' answered Garrett. 'We'll go to the cottage, pick up your kit. I'll pack and we'll throw a tent and some sleeping bags in as well. Pick up some supplies on the way. Maybe dig out one of my old jackets for you.'

An hour later the two friends were on the road and heading north.

As they drove Petrus marveled at the color of the surrounding landscapes.

'I've never seen so much green in my life,' he commented. 'Even though it's winter and so much of the place is covered in snow. I swear, I reckon that you could spit on the ground here and it would grow.'

'True,' agreed Garrett. 'If the snow or the frost didn't kill it first.'

They stopped at a supermarket and Garrett stocked up on food and drink. Petrus made sure that they had at least half a dozen bottles of cognac.

'After all,' he said 'We are actually on holiday.'

They arrived at their destination early that evening, driving the last couple of hours in the dark along barely visible game tracks.

There were no fences or obvious borders but Garrett knew the area so well, he could visualize where the laird's boundaries lay. He ground the Land Rover through the scrub until they came to a small, fast running stream where he parked next to a flat area covered in short heather.

Garrett turned the engine off and the two of them proceeded to set up camp. A brisk breeze blew from the north-east and flurries of snow eddied about them as they worked. But they were both experienced outdoorsmen and within a short time they had erected the tent, started a fire and built a windbreak from woven hanks of grass and twigs.

They broke out the cognac and sat close to the fire, drinking from mugs and smoking cigars, talking of inconsequentialities until the cold drove them into the tent and to sleep.

The next day they rose early and tramped the hills all day. Garrett noted down any game that he saw, and they came across two old, ramshackle crofter's cottages. The one was still vaguely livable but the other had succumbed to the elements and the roof had fallen in completely.

'Why doesn't anyone farm the land here?' asked Petrus. 'Couldn't laird Brody rent out the cottages?'

'Maybe,' admitted Garrett. 'But life is harsh this far north. Cold winters, short summers. Many years ago, people did lease the land. They used to breed sheep. But even then, the sheep were always sold on to lowlanders to fatten up. It's too hard up here to fatten the livestock, and crops don't grow well due to the frozen ground. So, the place is pretty much left alone. The laird uses it every now and then when one of his friends wants to rough it a bit, also for bow hunting and there's good salmon fishing in the lochs.'

'So, no one lives here?'

Garrett shook his head. 'Why.'

'I thought that I smelled wood smoke,' said Petrus. 'Just the faintest whiff. Coming from that direction.'

'There is an old croft that way,' said Garrett. 'It was still in quite good nick when I last saw it, maybe three years ago. But no one lives there. However, we better check it out, might be a bush fire.'

Petrus shook his head. 'I can smell the difference between a wood fire and a grass fire. Still, it was very faint. Maybe I imagined it.'

'Well, we can head that way and take a look,' continued Garrett. 'I'm sure that it's nothing but we can check out the cottage, maybe even shelter there for the night. Come on, let's trek.'

As they walked Petrus let his eyes rove across the landscape, cutting and quartering as they did so. Grid searching.

Garrett noticed and he called a stop, dropping to one knee and beckoning to Petrus to follow suit.

'What's wrong?' asked Garrett.

The Zulu shook his head. 'I don't know.'

'You're acting like we're on patrol in enemy territory. Why?'

Again, Petrus simply shook his head. 'A feeling. That's all.'

Garrett remained where he was for a while and he thought. Between Petrus and himself they had participated in more than two decades of combat. They had been wounded over thirty times, many of those wounds bringing them close to death. They had survived fire fights, land mines, plane crashes and countless assassination attempts.

But they were both still alive, while many of their past compatriots were long dead.

And Garrett knew, beyond any shadow of a doubt, that a large part of their continued longevity was due to the fact that they never, ever, ignored their feelings.

If Petrus felt that there was something wrong – well, that was good enough.

'Right,' said Garrett as he opened his pack and took out his machete. 'We continue to the same point but we get off the trail. We go covert. Eyes and ears open.'

Petrus nodded and he drew his assegai. 'Hey,' he whispered to Garrett. 'It's probably nothing, you know. I'm the first to admit that I'm one hundred percent paranoid.'

'True,' admitted Garrett. 'But just because you're paranoid, doesn't mean that they're not out to get you.'

Petrus grinned and the two of them continued forward.

Except now they were almost impossible to see, even if you knew that they were there. Two shades flitting through the gorse and the heather. A trick of the light. Perhaps an eddy of snow. A patch of shadow cast by a passing cloud.

They ghosted towards their destination, heading for the old croft cottage with all senses alert. After a few minutes Garrett raised his clenched fist and they stopped.

He put his mouth next to Petrus' ear and whispered softly. 'In front of us. Two o'clock. Next to the rock.'

Petrus looked and nodded. It was a man. That in itself was not what had caused the tension in Garrett's voice. What had caused it, was the fact that the man was obviously trying hard to conceal himself. And he was making a very good job of it.

'Why is he hiding himself?' whispered Petrus.

'There can be only three reasons,' answered Garrett. 'Either he is hiding from a pursuer, or he is part of an ambush or, finally, he is keeping watch.'

The two of them scanned the surrounds for over a minute and then Petrus spoke.

'It's not an ambush,' he said. 'Unless it's a one-man ambush, because there's no one else around. Also, he's not hiding from a pursuer. If he was, he would be further back into the gorse. He's keeping as much line of sight open as he can. He's a sentry.'

'I agree,' said Garrett. 'Can you see a weapon?'

Petrus shook his head.

'Me neither. So, he's probably not part of some military exercise. Logic dictates that he's keeping a watch out for people approaching the old croft. Let's give him a wide flank, come in from the other side and see if there are any more of them.'

Petrus nodded and the two friends slipped off into the shimmering mists of the gloaming. Wraiths amongst the living. They skirted round the sentry and approached the croft cottage from the opposite side. As they got closer, they spotted one other sentry. The man was situated on the top of a stac or small rocky mound. He was also well concealed and scoping out the surrounds.

By now the sun had completely gone down and darkness cloaked the land.

They were situated about a hundred yards from the croft cottage.

Petrus pointed at the chimney that protruded from the thatched roof. There was a tiny wisp of smoke curling from the top.

'Told you,' he said. 'Wood smoke.'

'Right,' said Garrett. 'I'm going to take a closer look. You cover me from here. If one of the guards makes a move to come back, delay him.'

'How?'

Garrett shrugged. 'I don't know. Use your imagination.'

Petrus nodded and Garrett disappeared into the dark, heading towards the cottage.

A few minutes later he had reached the back wall and he crawled along the ground, keeping in the deeper shadows until he got to the first window. Then he popped his head up and stole a quick glance inside.

He couldn't see the entire room but it looked like the dwelling was set out much like his cottage at home. A single room with a bathroom and toilet off it. There was no kitchen, merely a large open fireplace. The room was lit by the light of a small fire and two gas lamps, their harsh white light casting a mass of dancing shadows about the room as they hissed and flickered.

There were four camp beds set up and a rickety wooden table. A pile of olive, military issue bergens or rucksacks were piled in the corner. When he saw them Garrett swore under his breath. The reason for his ire was the fact that the bergens were not the standard issue 42's. Instead, they were the 72's, also known as SAS or PARA Bergen.

His initial assumption that these men were not military had been incorrect. Not only were they part of the military, it now seemed likely that they were in fact, a part of the military elite.

He moved slowly and silently across to the next window and peeked in. There were two men in the room and they both stood close to the fire, mugs of tea in their hands, not talking. They both sported close cropped military style haircuts and carried themselves with an erectness and confidence that reeked of military training.

Sitting on one of the beds was a young girl, perhaps eleven or twelve years old. She sat with her hands between her knees, leaning forward. It was obvious that she had been crying, her eyes puffy and red and her face still streaked with partly dried tears.

One of the men turned to her. 'You want some tea?'

She looked up at him and Garrett could see that, although she had been crying and her posture was one of defeat, her eyes were full of both anger and defiance.

'Fuck you,' she said.

He shook his head. 'You are a very impolite little girl,' he responded.

'And you are a psycho, child kidnapping piece of crap,' she snapped back.

The man walked over to her, mug of tea still in his one hand, and he causally back handed her across her face.

Her head snapped backwards and she was hammered sideways onto the bed.

'Maybe that will teach you some manners, you little shit,' shouted the man.

The girl struggled to rise but the blow had been too heavy and her head lolled back as she fell to the bed again.

Garrett's breathing quickened as his temper rose. And, in the dark recesses of his mind, the Beast awoke and started to growl.

The man grabbed the girl by the throat and squeezed. Her eyes bugged out and she thrashed about as she tried to free herself.

'Hey, Jackson,' said the other man. 'Careful. We need her alive.'

The man called Jackson loosened his grip and threw the girl to the floor. 'Just instilling some discipline,' he said with a laugh. 'Stupid bitch needs some.' He kicked her in the stomach and then took another sip of his tea.

And the Beast roared and threw itself at the bars that kept it in check, slavering and snarling.

But Garrett struggled for control. These were obviously British soldiers. They were meant to be the good guys. The whole thing just didn't compute and his emotions were at odds with themselves.

Then the girl whimpered in pain as she tried valiantly to sit up. Jackson flat handed her on the top of her head, knocking her back down, giggling as he did so.

The Beast smashed down its door and stepped out into the open.

Garrett adjusted his grip on his machete and ghosted around to the front of the cottage. He had no plan and there was little thought involved. The girl was an innocent. The men were bad. Garrett was there.

He simply smashed through the front door as if it were mere plywood and stepped into the room. A figure from a nightmare, his blade glowing dull red from the fire, his eyes wide and dark and full of malevolence.

But these were no ordinary men who stood before him and they both reacted instantly. Jackson threw his hot tea at Garrett and ran at him while the other man drew a short knife from his belt and moved to flank the intruder. Both men moved with confidence and economy of movement, secure in the knowledge that they were the best of the best.

But they had never faced the Beast.

Garrett swung his machete in a tight arc, his arm moving faster than the eye could see and he caught Jackson on the temple with the flat of the blade. Jackson went down like he had been head shot, hitting the floor like a sack of wet earth.

The second man approached in a more wary fashion, keeping his blade low, weaving it back and forth like a snake charmer's flute. It was an old knife fighting trick. A way of using movement to distract your opponent.

Garrett totally ignored it, keeping his eyes on the man's center mass. His torso. Because that is the area that telegraphs a man's movements before all others. People would have you believe that you watch a man's eyes, or his hand, or even his feet. But Garrett had learned that the body was the window to a combatant's movements.

The two men faced each other for almost a minute, watching and waiting.

In a knife fight there are usually only two movements. And after that, one of the combatants is bleeding and the other isn't. It is a form of combat that is quick and scary and deadly.

'Put the blade down,' said Garrett, his voice harsh with adrenalin. 'Put it down and walk away while you still can.'

The man shook his head. 'You first.'

Garrett took a deep breath. 'Come on,' he urged. 'There is no need for you to go here. Leave now or accept the consequences.'

The man smiled. 'You have no idea who you are dealing with,' he said as he lunged forward.

The machete swept down and connected, severing the man's hand from his wrist in one blow. Both hand and knife fell to the floor. Garrett reversed his blow and flicked the blade back, slicing through the man's throat as he did so. He was dead before his body hit the floor.

The Beast threw back his head back and howled.

He sensed movement behind him as someone ran in through the doorway and he raised his machete, ready to strike.

'It's me,' shouted Petrus.

'Where are the sentries?'

'I took care of them.'

'Dead?'

'I knocked the one unconscious but the other fought back hard. Things got out of hand.'

Garrett could see that Petrus' assegai was stained a dull red and that provided the answer to his question. One of the sentries was undoubtedly extinct.

'What the hell happened here?' asked Petrus.

'The girl,' said Garrett. 'They've kidnapped a little girl. He was hitting her,' he pointed at the unconscious figure of Jackson as he talked.

'What girl?' prompted Petrus.

Garrett cast his eyes about the room. There was no sign of the young girl.

'She's here,' he said. 'Must be.'

He started to pick the camp beds up and cast them aside. The girl was lying under the second bed and she screamed as he exposed her.

'Don't be scared,' said Garrett as he sheathed his machete. 'We're here to help you. We won't do you any harm. I promise.'

The girl stared at him, wide eyed, her whole body shaking in terror, as if she were undergoing the final stages of hyperthermia.

'You killed him,' she whispered.

'Yes,' admitted Garrett. 'I didn't mean to. I'm sorry.'

She shook her head. 'Don't be. He was an asshole.'

'Garrett,' called out Petrus. 'Lights coming. Land Rover. I suggest that we get the hell out of here.'

Garrett nodded. 'Can you move?' he asked.

The girl nodded.

'Come on then.'

The three of them left via the front door and Petrus led the way with the girl in the middle and Garrett bringing up the rear.

Petrus led them around the hill and away from the cottage in the opposite direction the lights were coming from. In deference to the young girl, they moved at a slow trot.

'They're going to come looking for us,' said Petrus as they ran. 'Maybe I should stay behind. Slow them down a bit. Discourage them.'

'No ways,' said Garrett. 'This has already gone too far. This is the United Kingdom, not Sierra Leone. We've killed two people. Whatever happens we are both in big shit, no matter how this plays out. Jesus, I chopped a guy's hand off and cut his throat.'

'I gutted my one,' said Petrus.

'You gutted him?'

'Yep,' affirmed the Zulu. 'Like a fish.' He chuckled.

'It's not funny, Petrus,' snapped Garrett. 'Even if those guys were kidnappers and child molesters, we will probably both end up going to jail for what we did.'

'Why?'

'Because you can't simply kill people here.'

'Fuck them,' growled Petrus. 'They try to put me in jail, I'll kill a lot more of them.'

'Look, for tonight we run, we hide. Head that way,' pointed Garrett. 'There's a small cave system there, we can spend the night there. No ways will they find us. Then tomorrow we go to the cops and report this. I'll try to keep your name out of it.'

'Whatever,' shrugged Petrus.

They jogged on in silence for a few minutes and then the young girl stumbled and fell. She got up quickly, but it was obvious that she was utterly exhausted.

Garrett cursed himself for being so unobservant.

'Come on, sweetheart,' he said and he picked her up in his arms as he ran.

'I'll be fine,' she argued.

'Sure you will,' said Garrett. 'But I'll just carry you for a while, okay?'

She nodded and closed her eyes. Within minutes she was fast asleep.

The two warriors sped up; breaking into a fast lope and an hour later they were ensconced in the small cave system that Garrett had talked about.

Petrus took first watch. He woke Garrett two hours later.

'No sign of anyone,' he whispered.

Garrett nodded and took over.

The young girl slept on solidly without moving.

CHAPTER SIX

An hour before sunrise, Garrett had left Petrus looking after the young girl and he had run around the perimeter of the laird's holdings, finding his way back to the Land Rover.

He drove the transport close to the caves and then went to fetch his friend and the girl.

They made their way back to the transport, clambered in, and Garrett set off for the nearest village with a decent sized police station.

'We'll head for Carrbridge,' he said. 'Probably stop at Moy, there's a cop shop there with more than a single Bobby in it. That's the place to go.'

'If you say so,' said Petrus.

'I do,' continued Garrett. 'Should take us about half an hour to get there. Now, my girl. First things first, are you feeling alright? Would you like a drink of water or something to eat?'

The girl shook her head.

'I'm Garrett. This here is Petrus. Your name?'

'I'm Lindsey. Lindsey Parker. I'm from Islington in London. Those assholes kidnapped me three days ago, drugged me up and brought me here. Wherever here is.'

'Here is Scotland,' said Garrett.

'Can I use one of your phones?' She asked. 'I need to phone my dad.'

'I don't have a phone,' admitted Garrett. 'Used to, but it broke and I didn't replace it.'

Petrus shrugged. 'Don't look at me, I'm on holiday. Why would I need a phone?'

Lindsey rolled her eyes. 'What are you guys, Amish or something? Who doesn't carry a bloody phone nowadays?'

'You can phone him at the police station,' said Garrett. 'It won't be long now.'

Lindsey nodded and lay back in her seat.

'Why did those guys kidnap you?' asked Petrus.

'I don't know,' snapped Lindsey. 'I'm not Sherlock Holmes.'

Petrus grinned. 'Maybe we take you back and see if they can sort your smart mouth out for you. You think?'

'I'm sorry,' apologized Lindsey in a small voice. 'It's just that I've had a shitty few days.'

'How old are you?' asked the Zulu.

'Twelve. Well, eleven. Almost twelve.'

'You swear too much for an eleven almost twelve-year-old, you know that?'

Lindsey shrugged. 'I hang around with older people most of the time.'

'Why?'

'I'm sort of a child genius.'

'Really?' asked Petrus the disbelief evident on his face.

'Yes really, mister doubting Thomas. IQ of 145, already been accepted into Oxford, start in two years time. Advanced mathematics.'

'Impressive,' admitted Petrus.

'Maybe I'm lying,' quipped Lindsey.

Petrus shook his head. 'Maybe, but I don't think so.'

'What does your father do?' asked Garrett.

'He's a science geek,' answered Lindsey. 'Lectures at Oxford, does some work for private companies.'

'Is he wealthy?'

She shook her head. 'No way. He inherited some money. Enough to pay off the house. Not enough to get a new car.'

'And your mother?' continued Garrett.

'And my mother nothing,' said Lindsey. 'She walked out on us six years ago. Spoken to her maybe four times since. She's a right bitch.'

'This doesn't make any sense,' said Garrett. 'There must be a reason that they kidnapped you. And a bloody good reason considering all the trouble that they went to.'

'Whatever,' said Lindsey. 'I just want to phone my dad and go home.'

'Well, we're almost there,' said Garrett as they drove into the small town and he headed for the high street. 'The cop shop is down here.'

He navigated down the high street and then pulled in, opposite the police station. It was situated in an old Victorian building. Red brick, large windows and a blue double door. Outside the main doors, attached to the wall with a curly Victorian metal bracket, was an old-fashioned blue lamp with the words, 'Police' painted in white on the glass.

'Wait here,' he instructed Petrus and Lindsey. 'I'm going to have a chat, then I'll call you in.'

'I'll come with,' said Lindsey.

'No, stay.'

'Fuck that,' cursed Lindsey. 'I want to phone my dad.'

'Language,' laughed Petrus.

'Okay,' said Garrett. 'Why not? Petrus, you stay here. I'm going to try to keep you out of this. Not sure if I can, but I will try.'

Garrett and Lindsey walked across the road and into the front of the police station. A small entrance area come charge office. Wooden bench against the one wall, a scratched and worn counter opposite. The walls painted a dull semi-gloss institutional green. Police information posters hung raggedly on the walls, tacked on with strips of yellowing sticky tape. 'Underage drinking is illegal', 'Blow the whistle on domestic abuse', 'No means no'.

There was no one at the counter. Garrett and Lindsey stood for a few seconds and then Garrett leaned over the counter and looked down the corridor behind it. That too was empty.

'I really need to phone my dad,' said Lindsey.

'Come on,' replied Garrett as he lifted the entrance flap on the counter and walked down the corridor. The rooms on either side of the passageway were all glass fronted and Garrett peered into the rooms as they walked past.

Then he stopped abruptly, grabbed Lindsey by the arm and dragged her back down the corridor, moving so fast that he literally pulled her off her feet.

'Hey,' she yelped. 'What gives? I need to phone my dad. Stop it.'

'Quiet,' hissed Garrett, his voice a command not to be ignored.

They went back through the counter and exited the building, still moving at a walk that bordered on a run.

Garrett bundled Lindsey into the back of the Land Rover, jumped into the front seat, started the engine and pulled off, heading out of town.

Petrus waited until they were clear of the traffic before he spoke.

'Trouble?'

'Big trouble,' affirmed Garrett.

'What?'

'That Jackson guy, the one that I cold cocked. He was in the station. Sitting in a room with another military type, and a cop. They were talking like they knew each other.'

'Shit,' exclaimed Petrus. 'We should have taken him out.'

'We can't just go around killing everyone,' disagreed Garrett.

'Why not?' asked Petrus. 'It's always worked for us in the past.'

'It's different here,' answered Garrett.

'Maybe he was reporting the fact that you guys attacked him and his friends,' suggested Lindsey.

'Never,' denied Garrett. 'No ways that he and his mates would go into a police station to report that the girl that they kidnapped was taken by someone else and they'd like to lodge a complaint.'

'True,' admitted Lindsey. 'Sorry. Stupid idea.'

'Gifted my ass,' said Petrus.

'Fuck you.'

'Language,' said both Garrett and Petrus at the same time.

They drove in silence for a few minutes and then Garrett took a right turn off the main road. He turned again soon after that and pulled off the road and down an old track, stopping the Land Rover behind a copse of trees so it was hidden from view.

'Right,' he said. 'What the hell is going on?'

Neither Petrus nor Lindsey spoke.

'Come on,' prompted Garrett. 'Any thoughts would be welcomed.'

'Okay,' said Petrus. 'Those guys that we came up against last night. You reckon that they're ex Special Forces?'

Garrett shook his head. 'Judging by their ages I'd say that they are current special forces. Their bergens were latest issue and looked relatively new. And you can't buy that stuff at the military surplus store.'

'Cool,' continued Petrus. 'So, we got the military and the cops in this thing, whatever this thing is, working together. Now, is it just the local cops or is it more widespread?'

'When those dickheads took me there was cop with them,' piped up Lindsey. 'I was at home alone, he knocked on the door. That's why I let them in.'

'What cops?' asked Garrett. 'London cops? Cops from up here?'

Lindsey shook her head. 'I don't know. Cops are cops.'

'Think,' urged Garrett. 'Anything that could help. It's important.'

Lindsey closed her eyes as she tried to remember everything about the incident.

'When he knocked on the door, I asked for him to show his badge at the peephole.'

'Did he?' Asked Garrett.

She shook her head. 'No. He said that they don't carry badges but he could show me his warrant card. He held it up.' Lindsey's brow furrowed in concentration. 'It had some Latin on it. Domine Dirige Nos.'

'You remember that?' asked Petrus sceptically.

'Yep,' affirmed Lindsey. 'Brain the size of a planet. Told you. It means...'

'Lord Guide Us,' interjected Garrett. 'It's the motto for the City of London police,' murmured Garrett. 'This is not good. What rank was he?'

Lindsey shrugged.

'On his shoulder, what badge did he have?'

'A crown, I think,' answered Lindsey. 'No, wait…a wreath.'

'Commander,' said Garrett. 'The equivalent of an army brigadier. Whatever this is, it's not only local and it goes pretty high up. Shit. Shit, shit, shit.'

'So what now?' questioned Petrus.

'We take Lindsey home.'

'Can't we stop somewhere so that I can phone my dad?' asked Lindsey. 'I want him to know that I'm okay.'

Garrett shook his head. 'Sorry, love. This thing is bigger than we all thought. I'd rather not phone ahead just in case. We'll drive to your house, get some eyes on. Take it from there. It won't be long, a few more hours.'

Lindsey didn't look happy but she trusted Garrett's logic.

Garrett started the Land Rover, slotted it into gear and drove off, heading for London.

CHAPTER SEVEN

As always, the traffic in London was a solid, crawling nightmare. The sun had gone down and the city was a sparkle of lights that reflected off the wet surfaces and fractured against the light rain like a scattering of multicolored jewels.

With Lindsey giving directions, Garrett wended their way through the ancient streets of the modern city until they reached Islington, a burrow of London.

As they approached the young girl's house, she started to become visibly excited at the prospect of seeing her father again.

Garrett took the final turn into her road and Lindsey pointed at her house.

'There,' she said. 'The Georgian house. Number thirty-seven.'

Garrett slowed down but continued driving on to the end of the road where he turned right and then pulled in some two hundred yards further on.

'Hey,' exclaimed Lindsey. 'What was the point of that?'

'There's a black cab parked outside the house.'

'So what?' asked Lindsey. 'There are black cabs all over London. It's famous for its black taxis.'

'Yeah, I know. But the driver was smoking and he had a flask of tea or something. Cabbies don't smoke in their cabs.'

'Maybe this one does,' argued Lindsey.

'We need to find a phone,' said Garrett. 'This is your neighborhood, any idea where a pay phone is?'

Lindsey shook her head. 'Why would I know that? Who the hell uses pay phones? There probably aren't any.'

Garrett pulled back into the flow of traffic and drove around the area in a random pattern looking for a phone box. Eventually they found a bank of three. He parked, climbed out with Lindsey and went over to them.

The first two were broken, the receivers pulled off and the units smashed. The third one was still intact and when Garrett picked up the receiver, he heard a dialing tone.

'Right,' he said. 'What's your number?'

'I'll phone,' said Lindsey.

'No. I'll phone. Give me your number.'

Lindsey recited a number and Garrett loaded fifty pence into the coin slot and dialed.

'What's your dad's name?' he asked as the phone rang.

'Bradley,' she answered. 'His friends call him Brad.'

There was a click and someone picked up the phone. They didn't say anything but Garrett could hear their breathing on the line.

'Hello,' greeted Garrett. 'Is that Brad?'

Still the man did not respond.

'Brad,' continued Garrett. 'Is that you?'

'Who is this?' asked the man. His voice was gruff. The accent pure London cockney.

'A friend of Brad's,' answered Garrett. 'From the university. Can I speak to him?'

'What's your name?'

Garrett placed the phone back in its cradle. 'How does your dad talk?' he asked Lindsey.

'What do you mean?'

'Your dad, what accent does he have?'

'He's posh,' said Lindsey.

'Well then your dad isn't there. The dude who answered the phone spoke like a barrow boy from the market. Rough as old bags.'

'So where is my dad?'

'I don't know, sweetheart,' answered Garrett. 'But I promise you, we will find out.'

They both went back to the Land Rover and he told Petrus what had transpired.

'Simple,' said Petrus. 'We sneak into the house, grab the dude inside and smash him up until he tells us what's going on.'

'We can't do that,' said Garrett. 'What if he's some sort of long lost relative, or some innocent cop or something?'

'Well, after we work him over, we'll know,' argued Petrus.

'Whatever we do,' said Garrett. 'We need to get Lindsey to a safe place.'

'Where?' asked Petrus.

'Maybe the laird's place.'

Petrus shook his head. 'No ways. Too many dick heads there. The laird's okay, but that fucking Alicia is a mental case and who know what other morons the laird might have to stay.'

'True,' admitted Garrett reluctantly.

'Hey,' interjected Lindsey. 'I'm not going anywhere. I want to stay with you guys. That's the safest. Anyway, you two need me.'

'Why?' asked Petrus.

'Because I'm the brains of the operation.'

'We'll get by,' argued Petrus.

Lindsey shook her head. 'Not so sure about that. I mean,' she pointed at Garrett. 'This one thinks he's Rambo, and you...well, you carry a spear, for fuck sakes.'

'Don't swear,' snapped Petrus.

'Sorry. But seriously, guys. Please don't make me go.'

'Okay,' said Garrett. 'We stick together. First, we better find a place to stay. Down market place that encourages cash payments. Lots of foreigners. Two rooms or some sort of family room. I reckon Earl's Court is a good place to start.'

Garrett pulled off and headed west. After a few wrong turns and an hour of crawling through traffic they cruised past the Earl's Court Exhibition Center. He drove slowly through the surrounding streets until he saw a hotel that caught his eye.

A row of faded Georgian houses that had been converted into a combination of single room apartments and one- and two-star hotels. Flaking paint, flickering backlit neon signs and ostentatious names.

He chose the third hotel along that went by the name of 'Grand Castle Hotel'. It sported a faded red and white flag outside with some sort of company logo, a neon sign that read, 'family rooms available' and a brass plaque boasting two stars. A hand written sign on the front door informed guests that there was Free WiFi.

'This is the place,' stated Garrett. 'Petrus, you got money?'

'Yep. About six hundred pounds.'

'Good, book a family suite with two rooms, or two separate adjoining rooms. Pay cash, give false names. Look, the likelihood is that no one is actually looking for us. Maybe for Lindsey, but not us. Still, don't take a chance. I'm driving back to my cottage in Scotland. I'm going to pick up a bunch of cash so we can go totally off grid.'

Petrus and Lindsey got out of the Land Rover and Garrett pulled off.

'Jesus Christ,' said Lindsey. 'What a fucking dump.'

'Sorry, princess,' said Petrus. 'Next time we'll stay at The Ritz.'

'Don't call me princess,' snapped Lindsey. 'I hate that.'

Petrus laughed and they went up the stairs and into the hotel.

CHAPTER EIGHT

Theoretically it is fairly simple to build an atomic bomb, provided one has a sufficient quantity of weapons grade plutonium.

And while plutonium is extremely difficult to obtain in any sort of adequate amount it is possible, with the right connections, to get hold of Plutonium Dioxide, the waste material; from a nuclear power plant. This can be converted into plutonium metal using a relatively simple chemical process.

Then, you basically make a plutonium sphere about four inches in diameter. You surround this with a shell of dense material, such as lead. This is called a tamper.

About 900 pounds of plastic explosive, molded around the tamper and placed around the sphere of plutonium, should be sufficient to compress the plutonium to the required degree.

A large number of detonators (say, about 50) must be inserted symmetrically into the plastic explosive so that the distance between each detonator and the surface of the plutonium sphere is constant.

When the high explosives are detonated, the shock waves cause the tamper to collapse inwards. The tamper's inertia helps hold together the plutonium during the explosion to prevent the premature blowing apart of the fissioning plutonium and thereby obtaining a larger explosion.

This would be likely to give a roughly symmetrical shock wave to compress the plutonium sphere. It is very possible that such a device would explode with an explosive power between fifty and a hundred tons of TNT.

Enough to devastate a large part of inner-city London.

Practically – this is not that easy to achieve.

When creating a nuclear weapon, measurements like 'about four inches,' and 'fifty or so detonators' are not accurate enough.

Exact critical mass of the blast material has to be calculated, the detonation has to be incredibly precise and the manufacture of the sphere and tamper has to be accurate within microns.

It is not something that a DIY expert could do in his garage.

No – to successfully construct a workable nuclear bomb you would need someone like Bradley Parker. A man with degrees in nuclear physics, engineering and pure mathematics.

As well as that, the man would either have to be a complete psychopath, or a fanatic of some sort.

Or he would have to incentivized in some major way.

Professor Parker was highly motivated to do as he was being told. Because the professor loved his daughter more than life itself. He would do anything, commit any atrocity and break any law to keep her from harm's way.

And he knew that they had her under lock and key, fully prepared to hurt her if he even contemplated disobeying them.

So, he put his head down and he worked.

He worked as slowly as he could without being obvious, and he asked for many materials that he actually did not need, but he still did all that he was instructed to do.

CHAPTER NINE

G arrett arrived back on the evening of the next day. He had driven all day, all night and then all through the next day and he was exhausted.

Before he went upstairs, he picked up a bag of Big Macs and fries and a few bottles of soda. Then he asked the reception which room Petrus was in and he went up.

He knocked on the door and called out at the same time.

'Hey, Petrus it's me. Open.'

Petrus opened the door.

'How you doing?' he asked.

'Knackered,' responded Garrett. 'Eat and sleep is what's needed.'

He threw the bag of burgers onto one of the beds alongside the packet of soda cans. Then he chucked a pile of newspapers down next to them.

'I brought some burgers. Also picked up about ten newspapers, local Scottish and national. There's no mention of our escapades in the highlands. So, I suppose that's good. And bad.'

'Why bad?'

'Proves that it's some sort of big illegal conspiracy. Oh well, whatever. How are you?' he asked Lindsey.

'Hi,' she chirped. 'I'm fine. Bored, but fine.' She picked up the bag of burgers and grimaced. 'Oh no,' she said. 'That's all that he buys as well. Bloody burgers and soda. Breakfast, lunch and dinner.'

'What's wrong with that?' asked Petrus. 'Bread, meat, soda. All the major food groups. And it's just across the road.'

'Then he eats about fifteen of them, and gives me one.'

'You never want more than one, Princess,' said Petrus. 'I do offer.'

'Yeah, that's because they're shit,' said Lindsey. 'Haven't you guys ever heard about salad, vegetables, fruit? And don't call me Princess.'

'It's got lettuce in,' said Garrett.

Lindsey groaned and grabbed a burger and a can of soda.

Both Garrett and Petrus tucked in as well, looks of enjoyment on their faces.

After a few burgers Garrett spoke.

'We have got to figure out why these guys kidnapped you,' he said. 'Have you got any rich relatives? Uncles, aunts. Anyone?'

Lindsey shook her head.

'Anyone famous? Politicians, activists?'

Again, she shook her head. 'No. Trust me; I come from a small, boring family line.'

'And you say that your dad is simply a lecturer? What exactly does he do? What does he lecture?'

'Listen,' said Lindsey. 'If you or Barney Rubble here had a smart phone I could show you his web page at the university, but as you both seem to still use smoke signals to communicate, I can't really help. I mean, he's my dad, I'm not his employer.'

Garrett shook his head. 'You're a smart ass,' he said. 'Okay, I'll go and buy a smart phone.'

'Get the new Apple iPhone,' demanded Lindsey.

'I'll get a couple of the cheapest smart phones that you can get on a SIM only deal so that we can burn them if needs be,' he said as he left the room.

He returned half an hour later with three Nokia's, and three prepaid SIM cards.

'Got these at Tesco,' he said. 'They've got a twenty-four-hour shop just down the drag.'

Lindsey took them and turned them over in her hand. 'These are shit,' she pronounced.

'They'll do,' said Garrett. 'Now set them up, one each, and show me the info on your dad.'

Lindsey spent the next few minutes setting up the phones. 'What ring tone do you want?' she asked Garrett.

'Doesn't matter.'

'Sure it does,' said Lindsey. 'A ring tone says something about your character.'

'Just make it ring,' said Garrett.

'Boring. Okay, here, this is my dad's page on the university website.'

Garrett took the phone and looked at the screen.

Professor Bradley Parker

Oxford DPhil in Science and Technology of Fusion Energy (EPSRC CDT)

MSc theoretical physics

DPhil engineering physics

'This is one bright dude,' he noted.

'Told you,' said Lindsey.

'Still doesn't shine any light on why someone would want to kidnap you. If it's not ransom then it must be to exert pressure on your dad. You sure that he doesn't do any work for the government?'

'Hey it's not like dad and I sit around every night and discuss his job in detail. But I'm pretty sure he wouldn't do government work. He's just not that sort.'

'Listen, man,' said Petrus. 'All this speculation isn't going to work for us. We're not detectives. If you really want to get to the bottom of things then we need to do it our way. And before we do that, we had better be sure that there is no other route to go.'

'I don't know if we have any other choices left,' said Garrett.

'There are always other choices,' returned Petrus. 'We could take her to the cops and hope for the best. We could leave her with the laird and make things his problems. I mean, we could just leave her and let her fend for herself. There are always choices.'

'Fuck you, Tarzan,' snapped Lindsey.

Petrus ignored her. 'All that I'm saying, my friend,' he continued. 'Is that, once we start, you know where things will end up. You know as well as I do what will happen.'

Garrett nodded thoughtfully.

'What's he talking about?' asked Lindsey.

'Escalation,' answered Garrett. 'Once we step this thing up then there will be no turning back. Not for us, not for you, and not for your father.'

'Why?' insisted Lindsey.

'Let's just say that our methods, while often effective, may not be best suited to a first world environment. We tend to be a bit heavy handed at times.'

'What have we got to lose?' asked Lindsey.

Garrett raised an eyebrow. 'Everything,' he answered. 'Someone's got to do something, and it looks like we are the only ones who are stepping up at the moment.'

'Oh well,' said Petrus with a grin. 'There goes my relaxing holiday.'

'First I need some sleep,' said Garrett. 'Been awake for three days now and I'm out on my feet.'

Petrus pointed at a door. 'I got three rooms, all connected. That's yours through there. The other one is for the princess.'

'Who's your princess?' snapped Lindsey.

Garrett nodded his goodnights and went through to his room.

Lindsey left as well, closing her door behind her. When she looked at her bed, she saw a couple of paper bags on it. She walked over and tipped the contents onto the bedclothes.

There was a toothbrush, toothpaste, a set of two hair brushes, a pack of socks and cotton underwear from Marks, and Spencer's and a T-shirt. Petrus had obviously brought them for her when he was last out getting lunch.

She picked up the shirt and unfolded it. It was white cotton, short sleeves. On the front was a photo of Princess Leia from the original Star Wars movie. Printed underneath was the caption – "Don't call me Princess".

Lindsey smiled.

And then she lay down on the bed and wept softly until she fell asleep.

CHAPTER TEN

D ebra Haddock was an attractive woman. But that was not what one first noticed about her.

Her most noticeable attribute was the almost palpable aura of power that exuded from her. An air of command. A supreme confidence built from years of leading. Years of dedication. And years of complete self-belief.

She had gone to a girl's only private school, paid for by her father's earnings as a top barrister. After that she had been accepted into Corpus Christi College Cambridge where she had read Philosophy and finished with a first.

From there she had gone straight into politics working with the Tory party.

Over the years she had worked her way up to become a very influential back bencher. But she would never progress any further. Because, although she had the strength, the determination and the intelligence to progress – she lacked the human touch that allowed one to further their career in politics.

Debra Haddock simply did not have the charm to garner votes. Either from the public or within her own party. She was all cold power and no warmth. Her very own robotic efficiency had become her downfall and had scuppered her chances of ever becoming Prime Minister, her ultimate goal.

But if Debra was anything, she was both truthful to herself and pragmatic. So, realizing her weak points she had concentrated instead on amassing power. And now, although she was officially still a mere back bencher, she controlled more power, ran more lives and affected the running of the country more than most of the members of parliament.

And at this moment that power was concentrated on the man that sat opposite her. One Colonel Grant Peterson, Territorial SAS 21 also known as the SAS Artists Rifles.

'What do you mean, the girl is gone? I thought that you had your best men on it.'

'I did,' spluttered Colonel Peterson indignantly. 'And now two are dead and two are injured. One of them very badly, we're not sure if he'll survive.'

'Who did this?' asked Debra. 'Have we any idea?'

The colonel shook his head. 'No. The one attacker was a white male, six-foot, dark hair. The other one, my boys didn't see him.'

'Were your chaps shot?'

'No,' answered Colonel Peterson. 'Actually, this is where the whole thing gets a bit strange. My chaps have had a close look at the wounds and they reckon that the weapons involved were…' The colonel looked embarrassed.

'Come on,' urged Debra.

'It sounds unbelievable, but it seems a though the one man was killed by a sword and the other was disemboweled by a spear.'

Debra stared at the colonel for a few seconds before she reacted. 'Bullshit.'

Peterson shook his head.

'Don't shake your head at me,' hissed the politician. 'What are you trying to tell me? That Picts armed with claymores and spears are roaming the Highlands, killing our Special Force soldiers and stealing their prisoners?'

The colonel hung his head in shame. 'No one knew we were there,' he insisted. 'I can only put the attack down to some sort of coincidence.'

Debra shook her head. 'You know, Grant,' she said, using the colonel's first name. 'Please think before you speak. I can accept coincidences. They do happen. I can accept that two men happened to come across our hideout and that they may have made an attempt to rescue the girl. But what are the possibilities that two random men could actually achieve that when faced with four SAS soldiers? Four of the best killers on the planet. Tell me, colonel – what are the odds?'

'I see what you mean,' admitted Peterson.

'What are you doing about it, colonel?'

'I've sent another three men up there. They're busy combing the hills for them. If they're there, then my boys will find them. I guarantee it.'

'And if they are no longer there?'

Peterson shook his head.

'Exactly,' snapped Debra. 'Look, I'll need to bring Commander Hastings into this. The police can definitely help us here.'

She leant forward and dialed a number, placing the call onto speaker phone.

'Commander. Debra here,' she greeted.

'Hello, Debra. To what do I owe the pleasure?'

'The girl's escaped.'

There was a long pause

'Commander, I said that the girl has escaped.'

'I know. My men informed me earlier.'

'And why wasn't I told?' enquired Debra, her voice a study in outrage.

'I didn't want to bother you until I had followed up,' retorted the commander.

'I am not happy with that, Hastings,' snapped Debra. 'We need to find her. Also, we need to find out who took her. I'm afraid that we have very little information to go on. I'd like you to put out an APB on her. You know her name and description.'

'Can't do that, Debra.'

'Why the hell not?'

'Don't snap at me, minister,' argued Commander Hastings. 'Firstly, I think that you've been watching too many American movies. We don't have APB's. I could do an all-ports warning or APW, which circulates a suspect's description to airports, ports and international railway stations to detect an offender leaving the country. But are we worried that she'll be leaving the country? Probably not.

'Secondly, if I do that it'll be out of our hands. Every man and his dog will know about it. There is every chance that the free press will pick up on it and then if they do find her there is absolutely no guarantee that'll it will be one of our chaps. Could be anyone, and then, once again, it's out of our hands.

'Look, I have already gotten hold of all of my boys that are trustworthy and instructed them to get onto it. I'll put out feelers as to who might be involved. Also, I recommend that we get some military chaps to search the highlands, she is probably still there.'

'We've already put some men into the Highlands,' affirmed Debra.

'Right then, minister,' said Hastings. 'I'll get onto it. Rest assured. I will get hold of all of my trusted contacts, both in the force and in the media. We will find them.' He cut the call.

Debra stared at the colonel without speaking until he stood up, jammed his cap onto his head and left the room with a curt nod of his head in lieu of a goodbye.

CHAPTER ELEVEN

Lindsey woke up and had a long shower. Then she brushed her teeth, her hair and dressed with fresh underwear and socks and her new 'Princess' T-shirt.

She opened the interleading door into Petrus' room and walked in. The two men were sitting on the bed and there was a torn open bag of breakfast MacMuffins piled high.

Lindsey grimaced. 'Oh my god. More fast food.'

Petrus grabbed a bag from the bedside table and handed it to her without speaking. She opened it. Inside she found a tub of yoghurt, a carton of fresh fruit salad, a carton of orange juice, a straw and a set of plastic cutlery.

She smiled. 'Thanks.'

Petrus grinned. 'No worries, princess.'

For once Lindsey let the nickname slide.

'I've been thinking,' said Garrett. 'It seems as though we have little choice. Tactically speaking, we don't know shit from shinola. We don't know who kidnapped Lindsey. We don't know why. We have no idea where her dad is. We don't know how high or how deep this whole conspiracy goes. Although I reckon that it must be a relatively small contingent of people, corruption is far from endemic in the United Kingdom.'

'That's why I reckon that we start at Lindsey's house, go and smack the dude there around a bit,' ventured Petrus.

Garrett shook his head. 'No. Whoever he is, the likelihood is that anyone guarding a house will be so low down the totem pole that he won't know shit either. We've got to do something to negate these people. I think that the best plan would be to go to the media. We get this all out into the open and that will draw their claws. They can't kill us or Lindsey without drawing attention to themselves or coming out into the open. Plus, it will allow the non-corrupt cops to search for Lindsey's dad.'

'Sounds like a plan,' admitted Petrus.

'Right, Lindsey,' said Garrett. 'Could you go online, get a list of national newspapers, find out which one has the biggest circulation and then get hold of their contact details for me.'

Lindsey threw out a mock Nazi salute. 'Jawhol, mein Fuhrer,' she shouted. 'Your wish is my command.'

Garrett shook his head. 'Just do it, okay?'

The task took Lindsey less than five minutes. 'Here,' she said. 'Dial this number. It's for the SUN newspaper. Biggest circulation, not sure about its quality of journalism though.'

'Don't care,' answered Garrett. 'I'm simply looking for numbers.'

Garrett dialed the number, switched to speaker phone and lay the phone down on the small coffee table.

'Sun Newspapers, can I help?'

'I'd like to speak to a reporter,' said Garrett.

'What about?'

'I'd like to report a crime.'

'Phone the police sir.'

'No,' insisted Garrett. 'I need to speak to a reporter.'

'Well, sir, if you'd like to email us and give a brief synopsis of what you would like to discuss as well as a contact number, someone will get back to you shortly.'

'Listen lady,' growled Garrett. 'This is a genuine matter of life or death. I need to speak to a reporter right now.'

'Yes sir, fine. Please hold.'

The sound of super-soft Europop drifted from the speaker like a cloud of sleeping gas.

Garrett ate a MacMuffin and drank a soda. The muzak continued its attempt at sensory deprivation for another three minutes and then, without warning, the speaker went silent.

'Fucking assholes,' muttered Garrett. 'What's the next paper on the list?'

Lindsey gave him another number.

As the receptionist picked up the phone Garrett spoke before she could.

'Good day, this is detective inspector Partridge, Scotland Yard. I need to speak to the editor, Peter Soames immediately.'

'Oh, of course, sir,' said the receptionist. I'll put you straight through.'

Lindsey giggled and Garrett winked at her.

'Soames here, how can I help you, detective inspector?'

'Mister Soames, I'm sorry about the subterfuge, I'm not actually inspector Partridge. My name isn't important but I have some information regarding a young girl who has been kidnapped.

'Her father has also disappeared. We have no idea why the abduction took place. However, we have the girl, we are safe and we need to speak to a reporter.

'We suspect that elements of the police and the military are implicated and the only way to negate the rogue elements involved is to get this whole thing out in the open as soon as possible.'

The editor reacted like the true professional that he was, wasting no time on unnecessary questions. 'Right, I need to know where you are, and I'll send one of my top boys over to interview you.'

Garrett gave him the hotel name and address as well as his room number.'

'Don't leave the room. Give me an hour or so,' said Soames.

Garrett grunted an affirmative and then disconnected the call.

Soames replaced the receiver and stared out of the window for a while, taking in the view of the Kensington Gardens Square with its ancient trees and manicured lawns.

Then he picked up the telephone again and dialed a number from memory.

'Commander Hastings,' he said. 'Good morning. It's Peter Soames here. Listen, commander, I've just had a rather interesting phone call. I think that it may have been from those chaps that you phoned me about earlier today…'

S o,' said Lindsey. 'What do you guys do? I mean, when you're not sitting in dodgy hotel rooms gorging on hamburgers.'

'We save little girls from kidnappers,' answered Petrus.

'Ha and ha,' quipped Lindsey. 'Very humorous. No, seriously. What do you guys do for a living?'

'I'm a game warden,' said Garrett. 'Up in the Highlands. I run a laird's estate. Got a little cottage. It's good. Peaceful.'

'But that's not what you always did,' pointed out Lindsey.

'Why do you say that?' Asked Garrett.

'Because I'm not grotesquely stupid,' she quipped. 'I saw the way that you handled those shit heads that kidnapped me. You're some sort of ex-soldier or something.'

'Used to be a soldier,' admitted Garrett. 'But that was long ago and far away.'

'And you?' Lindsey asked Petrus.

Petrus shrugged. 'I drink beer. Sit in the sun. Watch the cows. Drink beer.'

'You said drink beer twice,' pointed out the young girl.

'I drink a lot of beer.'

There was a knock at the door and the two men stood up. Petrus moved across to the window and Garrett went to the door.

'Yes?'

'I'm from the newspaper. Mister Soames sent me.'

Garrett opened the door.

The man who stood there was no more than average height. Round, wire rimmed glasses, cropped gray hair. He was built like a tri-athlete, trim and wiry.

He held his hand out. 'My name is Bruce Campbell. Crime desk. May I come in?'

Garrett shook his hand and ushered him in.

He nodded to both Petrus and Lindsey. 'Good morning, sir. Lindsey.'

They both nodded back. Lindsey stayed sitting on the bed and Petrus remained by the window.

Bruce pulled back a chair and sat down at the small table. Then he took out a notebook and a pen. 'Right,' he said. 'Talk to me.'

Garrett told the reporter their story, keeping it succinct and to the point, starting with their discovery of Lindsey, the rescue and their subsequent escape.

Bruce nodded as he wrote. 'Yes,' he murmured. 'Very good. Impressive. Carry on.'

Garrett went on to tell him about seeing Jackson at the police station, how they then had to move on. The fact that they had phoned Lindsey's house and some unknown person had answered.

Petrus stayed at the window, twitching back the curtain every now and then and peering outside.

Bruce kept nodding and writing.

And then, without warning, the Zulu strode across the room and launched a massive blow at the reporter, smashing him off the chair and sending him crashing across the room and onto the floor.

Lindsey screamed and Garrett leapt to his feet.

'Jesus, Petrus. What the fuck?'

'He's a fake,' said Petrus. 'There are men outside, watching the place. I'm sure that they arrived with him.'

'So?' asked Garrett. 'They could be associates, bodyguards. Other reporters.'

'Then how come he knew Lindsey's name?' demanded Petrus.

'I'm pretty sure that I mentioned her name on the phone to the editor,' countered Garrett.

'You didn't,' stressed Petrus as he walked over to the man's unconscious body.

Lindsey nodded her agreement.

Then the Zulu rolled the body over and frisked it, pulling a small military-green pistol from his belt. He threw the weapon to Garrett. 'There, how many reporters carry those?'

Garrett looked at the pistol. 'It's a Walther P99, the new version of the old James Bond PPK.'

'What is this guy then?' asked Petrus. 'Some sort of spy?'

Garrett shook his head. 'No, the weapon is green, not black. So he's military. Most likely SAS, I think that this is their sort if kit. See this?' Garrett pointed to the end of the barrel. 'That's a thread to take a silencer, check the rest of his pockets.'

Petrus roughly checked and came up with an extra magazine and a silencer. He chucked them to Garrett.

Garrett pocketed the magazine and screwed the silencer onto the barrel. Then he slipped it into his belt, under his shirt in the small of his back.

The fake reporter started to mumble as he came to and Petrus tore some strips from one of the sheets and bound him to a chair.

'Okay, dude,' continued Garrett. 'Talk to me. Who are you?'

The man simply stared; his face expressionless.

Garrett turned to Petrus. 'Look, I've worked with these SAS fuckers before,' said Garrett. 'If he doesn't want to talk, then we simply don't have the time to break him. Trust me on this.'

Petrus sighed. 'I'm getting real sick of this shit,' he said. 'Take Lindsey next door. Give me a few minutes. He'll talk.'

As Garrett led Lindsey from the room, Petrus walked over to his rucksack and pulled out his assegai.

'Don't take too long,' urged Garrett. 'We don't know how long his mates will wait before they come looking for him. We need to move ASAP.'

Garrett closed the interleading door and started packing Lindsey's goods into a plastic shopping bag.

'What's Petrus going to do?' asked Lindsey in a small voice.

'Don't worry about it,' said Garrett. 'He's going to try to find out where your dad is, that's all.'

Lindsey sat down on the edge of the bed, her hands between her legs, her lips quivering slightly.

There was a sharp scream from next door that was cut off with the sound of a blow. Then a long-drawn-out sigh.

A few minutes later Petrus came through, closing the door behind him. 'You were right,' he informed Garrett. 'The bastard wouldn't talk.'

'Maybe I should give it one last try?' enquired Garrett.

Petrus looked embarrassed and shook his head. 'Sorry,' he said.

'Oh, dammit,' cursed Garrett. 'You…'

Petrus nodded.

'What happened?' asked Lindsey.

'Nothing,' answered Petrus. 'Oh, by the way. I can't see his mates on the street anymore. I'd say that they're probably on their way up to see us.'

'Shit,' said Garrett. 'This thing is starting to escalate quickly. And now that you've iced that guy, I very much doubt that his mates are going to give us a friendly reception.'

'So?' said Petrus. 'We wait, they come, we kill them, put a Do Not Disturb sign on the door and get the hell out of here.'

'No,' shouted Lindsey. 'You can't just go around killing everyone. What the fuck? Are you guys, complete psychos?'

'Don't swear,' chimed in Garrett and Petrus together.

'Don't swear,' said Lindsey in disbelief. 'You're fucking killing people.'

'Needs must,' said Petrus philosophically. 'Needs must.'

'Look,' said Garrett. 'I'm actually in agreement with Princess here. We've got to put some sort of lid on the situation. If we simply continue to ice all of these guys then all hell is going to break loose.'

'Hey, man,' said Petrus. 'I hate to state the obvious but all hell has already broken loose. I mean, do you honestly think that the asshole next door with the silenced pistol and all of his mates were here to negotiate? No ways, he was here to off us.'

'True,' admitted Garrett. 'But this isn't Africa. We start piling up bodies here and the whole world will come looking for us. I'm talking thousands of cops, CCTV cameras, road blocks, mobile phone tapping, other shit that we've never even heard of.'

Petrus shook his head. 'I disagree. If these guys were playing it straight and narrow, then they would have simply sent the cops here. Instead, they sent a hit squad. Also, by the way, how the hell did they know that we were here? The media must be in on this as well.'

'Scary, man,' commented Garrett. 'But I think that you're right. So, I reckon that we neutralize these guys and then get to Lindsey's house like you said, see if we can pick up any clues there.'

Garrett took out the pistol, checked the load, racked it and slipped the safety off.

'Ready to rock and roll,' he grunted. 'Petrus, stay here with Lindsey. I'll go back into the other room, that's where they'll come. I'll take them down in there.'

Garrett went through to the next-door room and dragged the dead body into the bathroom. Then he opened the front door, leaving it slightly ajar.

After that he simply went and stood in the middle of the room, waiting. Clearing his mind. Breathing in slow measured breaths.

Literally seconds later he heard steps in the corridor. Confident, considered. Three men. He continued waiting, at ease. Relaxed.

The men approached the door and stopped, seeing it was open.

Garrett had left the door ajar on purpose. Because, when a man is faced with a locked door that he has to kick open, his adrenalin is automatically ramped up. He becomes faster, more aggressive. Harder to kill.

But an open door is merely something to be pushed open. This inspires caution. Prudence becomes the prevailing emotion as opposed to aggression.

The door was pushed slowly open.

Three men came through, guns drawn. The same olive-green Walther P99's with suppressors on. They saw Garrett straight away and pointed their pistols at him and spread out.

Garrett did not move or react.

'Get down,' shouted one of the men. 'Do it. Now.'

Still Garrett didn't react; he simply stood rock still, staring straight ahead. Not blinking. Like he was in a coma. Or maybe meditating.

The three men moved slowly towards him, their weapons outstretched, ready to fire.

'What the fuck is up with this guy?' asked one of them as he took another step closer.

Now the three of them were grouped closer together. And their initial aggression had run down into something more akin to curiosity.

Garrett blinked, and time seemed to slow down as adrenalin flooded his system. Microseconds became full grown seconds. He could see the motes of dust as they danced in the shaft of light coming in through the dirty window. He could smell the mix of sweat and cheap deodorant and Old Spice aftershave on the three men. He could hear traffic outside. A man shouting, not English, maybe Italian, maybe.

He moved sideways, drawing the pistol as he did so, firing as soon as it reached the horizontal. Quick double taps.

Bangbang. Bangbang. Bangbang.

The noise still shockingly loud despite the silencer. Like a child throwing telephone books to the floor in a tantrum.

All three men went down.

Garrett stepped over to them, pointed the pistol again and fired a single round into each man's head.

The normal passing of time returned with a rush and Garrett took a deep breath. Then he closed the front door, hanging a 'do not disturb' sign on the handle as he did so. After that he searched the bodies, collecting up all three pistols and extra ammunition, and loaded them into his tog bag.

'Petrus,' he called as he knocked on the interleading door. 'It's me.'

The Zulu opened the door and Garrett walked in and passed the bag to Petrus.

'Three more pistols and ammo in there,' he said.

'Any ID on them?' asked Petrus.

Garrett shook his head. 'No, but they were soldiers. Their hair, their builds, the way they moved. Probably special forces.'

'Can't be that special,' quipped Petrus. 'You popped them all before they even got a shot off.'

'I said that they were special,' said Garrett. 'I didn't say that they were as good as me.'

'True,' admitted Petrus. 'Let's go. Come on princess.'

They left the building, eyes moving as both Garrett and Petrus kept alert for any possible unfriendlies as they walked to the Land Rover.

For once Lindsey was dead quiet, her face pale and her hands shaking.

Petrus put his arm around her and she leant against him, her eyes glazed with unshed tears.

Garrett opened the Land Rover doors, they climbed in and he pulled off.

CHAPTER THIRTEEN

Garrett walked out of the hardware store and went into the convenience store next door. After a few minutes he walked back to the Land Rover and got in.

'Here,' he said as he handed cans of cold soda to Petrus and Lindsey.

'What else did you get?' asked the Zulu.

'Plastic zip ties, duct tape and this,' Garrett pulled out a pair of nylon stockings. He handed one to Petrus. 'Disguise,' he said.

Petrus stretched his out. 'It's not really my color,' he complained.

Garrett laughed. 'Make do.'

Once more they drove past Lindsey's house, pulling into a back street around the corner. Then Garrett and Petrus left Lindsey in the Land Rover as they sneaked around to the back of her house, climbing through the adjoining gardens to do so.

Once they were outside the back door, they donned their stockings.

'I'm not sure if these guys are cops or military,' said Petrus. 'Better if they're cops, those SAS dudes just won't talk, no matter what you do to them. I reckon that the first thing we do is incapacitate the guy, zip tie him to a chair and then find out if he's a cop or not. Depending on his profession, we take it from there.'

'Okay,' said Garrett. 'We go in hot, guns out. But try to keep it quiet and keep initial violence to a minimum. If he's SAS then we tie him up, gag him and then search the house, see what we can find out. If he's a cop then we do bad guy, worse guy on him. Get him to talk.'

'Okay,' agreed Petrus. 'Should I be bad guy or worse guy?'

Garrett smiled. 'I reckon that we both try to outdo each other. But remember, this guy might just be an innocent cop, so keep damage to a minimum.'

They checked the back door. It was locked. Petrus drew his spear and slid it under the sash window in the kitchen. He popped the latch. They slid the window up and crawled through.

They ghosted through the house, out of the kitchen, down the corridor, past a few dark, empty rooms.

There was a faint light shining from a room near the end of the corridor and they peered through the door. A man sat at the dining room table. A single lamp in the room gave off light but the man had draped a cloth over it, probably a scarf, and it had cut the luminescence down to a low glow. He was reading a magazine.

He was also wearing a police uniform, on his upper arm the three yellow chevrons of a sergeant.

Garrett held up five fingers and the two friends counted down together.

On five they both rushed into the room. Petrus slapped a length of duct tape over the policeman's mouth and Garrett quickly zip tied his arms and legs to the dining room chair that he was sitting on.

Petrus stood in front of the cop and held his assegai in front of the man's face.

'Do you see this?' he asked.

The man stared, wide eyed at the weapon, but did not react.

'This is not a rhetorical question,' stressed the Zulu. 'Can you see this? Nod if you can?'

The man nodded frantically.

'Oaky,' continued Petrus. 'This is what is going to happen. I am going to ask you a question. Then I am going to take the tape off your mouth. You will answer the question. If you make any other noise, or if you say anything that does not pertain to the question, I will stab you with this spear. Do you understand?'

Again, the man nodded.

'Good. First question. What are you doing here?'

Garrett ripped the tape off the man's face. The cop immediately started to shout for help but before he got a whole syllable out Garrett had slapped the tape back on.

Petrus put his face close to the policeman and shook his head sadly. Then, without warning, he stabbed him in the bicep, the blade sinking in about two inches.

The cop thrashed around like he had been tasered.

Garrett pulled his friend aside. 'Hey, I thought that we agreed, keep bloodshed to a minimum.'

'I am,' argued Petrus. 'I mean, I didn't stab him in the eye, or gut him or anything like that. I only stabbed him in the arm. It's a flesh wound.'

'Don't be stupid,' said Garrett. 'All wounds are flesh wounds.'

'You know what I mean,' said Petrus. 'Anyway, let's get back to questioning him. I believe that he'll be more compliant.'

They went back to the man and stood in front of him. Garrett took the tape off and then went down on one knee so that his face was on the same level as the cop.

'What are you doing here?' He asked.

The policeman stared at Garrett with a look of hatred in his eyes and he said nothing.

Petrus sighed. 'Listen, dude,' he said. 'Do you want me to stick this in your eye?'

The man shook his head.

'Well then answer the questions, or I swear to you that I will blind you.'

The man nodded. 'Okay,' he said. 'I'm waiting.'

'For who?' asked Garrett.

'No one specific. The boss simply told us to wait and see who pitched up. We're meant to detain them for questioning.'

'Why?'

'I don't know.'

Petrus waved his assegai in front of the man's eyes.

'Don't do that,' blurted the cop. 'I'm serious. I'm just doing as I was told.'

'When do your replacements arrive? Yours and the guy outside.'

'Eight o'clock. Couple of hours.'

'Who is the boss? Who told you to stay here?'

'My immediate superior is Inspector Johnson, but the big boss is Commander Hastings. The Commander told us himself.'

Garrett looked at Petrus and the Zulu nodded. 'I reckon that he's telling the truth,' he said.

'I am,' insisted the cop. 'Promise. Don't stab me again.'

Garrett placed the duct tape back over the cop's mouth and then the two friends did a quick search of the house.

Nothing unusual came to light and Petrus spent some time loading up a rucksack full of clothes for Lindsey. On the way out he also grabbed her a warm coat from a coat rack in the corridor.

CHAPTER FOURTEEN

T he flickering sodium lights bathed the area in a sickly yellow glow, providing just enough illumination to pick out the broken windows, peeling paint and sagging chain link fencing. Light industrial, post-apocalyptic warehouse chic.

The Thames was visible through the rows of mostly abandoned buildings and the winter wind whipped off the river, banging at the unlatched doors and picking at the sheet metal roofs like a child scratching at a scab.

In the midst of the ramshackle industrial complex one building stood out. Not by virtue of being any less run down or well lit, merely by the fact that there were six vehicles parked outside. Three of them new executive model, upper middle-class, modern-day chariots. A silver Jaguar XF, a dark green Range Rover and a white Volvo XC90.

The inside of the warehouse totally belied its beaten exterior, the dilapidated shell housing a spotless array of rooms, painted in gleaming white, carpeted and polished to a military spec.

It was here that Bradley Parker was being held captive, figuratively chained to a laboratory as he endeavored to manufacture a nuclear bomb as slowly as he possibly could without raising suspicion and bringing his daughter to harm.

In a room only two away from the professor sat Minister Debra Haddock. Opposite her, looking decidedly less comfortable than the politician, stood Colonel Peterson and Commander Hastings.

Debra lit a cigarette, took a drag and then glared at the two men.

'I'm smoking again,' she said. 'Smoking. Do you know why?'

Both men shook their heads.

'The short answer is that I am surrounded by fools.' She glared at the police commander. 'Your boy let himself get tied up, stabbed and questioned. I thought that he was meant to apprehend them, not totally capitulate.'

'Steady on, Debra,' argued Commander Hastings. 'The sergeant knew nothing. Wasn't even in the loop. And there was no information in the house, we had already gone through it.'

'Still,' continued Debra. 'Small potatoes compared to the complete and utter fuck up you are in command of,' she snapped at the colonel. 'What the hell are you doing, Grant? First you lose the hostage, then the perpetrators are basically delivered to you on a plate and, not only do you lose them, you get another four of our men killed.'

Colonel Peterson cleared his throat. 'In all fairness, Debra. These men we are up against are different.'

'In all fairness, Grant,' taunted Debra. 'You are a complete penis.'

The colonel blushed a deep red, more from anger than embarrassment. But he held his tongue. He was used to military discipline and he well knew that shit always flowed downhill. And he was a step below the minister in the current setup.

Debra leaned forward and used her lit cigarette to point at the SAS colonel. 'Grant, how many men have you lost?'

'Six KIA, and one still in a coma.'

'How many inner circle men have you got left? And by that, I mean proper trustworthy men who know of the plan.'

'Five, maybe,' answered the colonel. 'But I could garner a few more if needs be. I have many true patriots in my regiment.'

'Well then I think that we can safely say that, for the immediate future, you are a spent force.'

'I object,' yelled the colonel. 'I may only have five men left but they are the very best of the best, Debra. The British SAS are not a force to be trifled with.'

'Spare me your histrionics, colonel,' returned the minister. 'That is exactly what has happened. Your men have been trifled with by two unknown strangers armed with swords and spears. I am not denigrating our famous Special Forces; however, I am saying that, perhaps, we need to fight this battle in a different way.'

Peterson looked slightly mollified and his high color faded to a more acceptable pink, as opposed to the rag-to-a-bull red that he had achieved before.

'What do you propose, Minister?' He asked.

'I'm going to bring in some outside help,' answered Debra. 'Don't worry, these men are consummate professionals. They have done work for our government before, MI5 mainly, and there is never any comeback. It will be rather expensive but, as you both know, we I have access to various government funds so that won't be a problem.'

'Who are these people?' asked Commander Hastings.

'It's a crowd that call themselves, 'The Custodians'. They're an executive mercenary outfit, ex Israeli MOSSAD and ex South African BOSS, Bureau of State Security. Really bad bastards, the head man goes under the moniker of 'The Curator'. The admin staff are 'Attendants' and the actual wet work specialists are called 'Watchmen'.'

'Can we trust them?' asked Peterson.

Debra shrugged. 'Probably more than most. As I said, they are completely mercenary. You pay the piper and he plays your music. But they will need complete cooperation from us,' she continued. 'Jarvis,' she addressed the police commander by his Christian name.

They will need everything that you have access to. CCTV, phone tracking, any word from the street.'

Jarvis nodded. 'I will relay it through you.'

As was her habit, Debra simply stared at the two men until they nodded their goodbyes and left.

She leant back in her chair and lit another cigarette. Sometimes it was difficult to hide her scorn that she felt for her two compatriots. At least they were keen and patriotic but their intelligence had much to be desired. But that was oft the case in most government positions, people tended to be promoted until they eventually reached a position that was beyond their capabilities. As such, that resulted in pretty much ninety nine percent of the country being run by leaders who were out of their depth. A veritable ship of fools.

However, that was a simple fact and there was little that she could, or indeed even wanted to do about it.

But there were many things that she could change. She could stop her beloved country kowtowing to the Europeans and the Muslims and the Germans. She could get rid of the benefit class by forcing them into the army. She could up the nation's military spending until it was at least on a par with the other countries in Europe and preferably way above them.

She could force people to admit that they were at war. Because Britain and her people were never so strong as when they were fighting a war, be it the Great War, the second world war, the Falklands or the Gulf.

Now they were fighting the greatest evil they had ever faced as the Muslim jihadists and ISIS radicals attacked not only the people of England but also their way of life and their very freedom.

And once she had shown the people the evil ways of the enemy, then she would galvanize them and lead them. Because they would need a leader. A leader chosen for their strength and ability as opposed to their sound bites and their airbrushed campaign posters.

They would need her.

Debra Haddock – Prime Minister.

She crushed her cigarette out in a small brass ashtray on the desk, took out her cell phone, dialed a number and left a message. One word. 'Yes.'

Debra knew that within twenty-four hours a package containing three unlisted mobile phones would be delivered to her home address. They would be set so that she would not be able to dial out on them. They would be receive-only.

The Custodians would phone her. Each phone would be used once and then the sim had to be removed and the phone discarded.

Haddock knew the system because she had used The Custodians once before and she had been impressed.

Very impressed.

CHAPTER FIFTEEN

T hey stayed the previous night in another down-market, single star hotel and took breakfast at a greasy spoon. A hole in the wall that catered for builders and firemen and other early morning risers who demanded a massive calorie intake to break their fast.

Garrett and Petrus had gone for the 'Full English', a large plate of fried eggs, sausage, bacon, mushroom, onion, beans, fried bread, toast and black pudding together with a mug of steaming, strong, sweet tea.

Lindsey had ordered a slice of buttered toast with a glass of apple juice.

Garrett ordered a second mug of tea and sat back in his chair. 'I've been thinking,' he said. 'No sarcastic comments please, Petrus.'

The Zulu laughed.

'Seriously,' Garrett continued. 'We need to find a more permanent place to stay. The more we move around, the more we expose ourselves. We need a safe house, something that is completely off the grid. Also, this thing is bound to keep escalating. And we need to cater for that, so we need to tool up. Get hold of some proper weapons to supplement these little Walthers that we have.'

'Easier said than done,' quipped Petrus.

'I know someone,' said Garrett. 'It's going to cost but I've got enough.'

'Okay,' said Petrus. 'I'll pay for the breakfast; you pay for the safe house and the weapons.'

'Sounds fair,' laughed Garrett.

After Petrus paid, they got into the Land Rover and Garrett headed for an area called the Elephant and Castle. A part of London that had yet to see any substantial gentrification. It was a place where the more street smart didn't use the underground walkways and they avoided walking around alone too long after dark. Tourist guide books described it as edgy, with a lot of state housing blocks and a high crime rate.

Garrett's contact lived in a large, ramshackle Victorian house that remained wedged between a multi-level car park and an office block. He pulled up outside and led the way to the front door.

'Listen,' he said. 'A word of warning. The bloke that we're about to see goes by the name of, The Scarlet Man. Petrus, you can call him Scarlet. Lindsey, you call him Uncle Scarlet, okay?'

'Why?'

'Just do it.'

Lindsey sighed. 'Lame. Alright. Why do they call him Scarlet?'

'Long story. Another time, maybe,' said Garrett. 'Oh yeah, he's old but thinks that he looks young, wears a goddamn awful wig. Just go with it and if he asks you how old he looks say thirty-five, maybe thirty-eight. Also, watch yourself with him. Don't cause offence, be respectful at all times.'

Lindsey shook her head. 'What's up?' she asked. 'You sound as if you're scared of him or something.'

Garrett looked at her before he spoke, his expression serious. 'Terrified,' he said softly.

He pressed a button on an intercom next to the door. Above him a CCTV camera whirred and turned in its protective wire cage, focusing on them.

Then there was a click and the door nudged open. He pushed it wide and walked in, gesturing for the others to follow him.

A man stood in the large, dark entrance hall. He stood around six feet six or seven, his shoulders impossibly wide tapering down to hips that seemed too narrow to support the bulk of muscle above them. He wore a deep purple suit, a cravat and patent leather shoes with spats. On his head perched a blue-black hairpiece that contained so much nylon in it that it crackled with latent static electricity when he moved.

When Lindsey looked closely at him, she could plainly see that he had affixed small squares of Scotch Tape to his temples and the top of his forehead, in order to pull back his wrinkles and tighten the skin on his face.

He had also applied a deep ocher shade of fake tan liberally all over his face and hands, but for some reason, had forgotten to color the back of his right hand which stood out like a dead appendage in an unpleasant fish belly white.

His teeth were perfectly capped little alabaster lozenges and his eyes a vivid blue that can only be achieved through the use of colored contact lenses.

For some reason he made Lindsey think of the Mad Hatter from Alice in Wonderland.

> *Twas brillig, and the slithy toves*
> *Did gyre and gimble in the wabe:*
> *All mimsy were the borogoves,*
> *And the mome raths outgrabe.*

He looked at her and smiled, and she felt a thrill of fear shudder through her as he did so.

'Garrett, my darling boy,' the man greeted the soldier, his voice a bolt of silk wrapped around a steel sword.

Garrett bowed low. 'Scarlet, thank you for receiving us. May I introduce my good friend, Prince Dinangwe, known also as Petrus Sizwe Dlamini, eldest son of chief Dlamini of Drummond, the Valley of a Thousand Hills.'

Petrus raised an eyebrow as he wondered what his friend was playing at, but he went with it and bowed as well. 'A pleasure to meet you, mister Scarlet.'

'And this,' continued Garrett. 'Is Lindsey Parker. We call her, Princess.'

Lindsey did a perfect curtsy. 'Uncle Scarlet,' she greeted, keeping her eyes downcast.

Scarlet leered at her. 'Charming,' he purred. 'Now, follow me.'

As they meandered through the large house it became obvious that many of the rooms were in use. They were afforded glimpses through doors left slightly ajar - red walls, tapestries, low lights and piles of silk cushions. The air was redolent with the smell of burning maple syrup and incense.

Lindsey wrinkled her nose in distaste.

'Opium?' asked Garrett.

'"Among the remedies which it has pleased Almighty God to give to man to relieve his sufferings, none is so universal and so efficacious as opium", I believe Thomas Sydenham said that,' quoted Scarlet. 'Physician, mid sixteen hundreds, Studied at Oxford, took thirty years to qualify as a medical doctor. Went on to discover St. Vitus' Dance. Prescribed the use of opium for pretty much every disease known to man. Very droll fellow, to say the least.'

'So you're running a drug den?'

'I prefer the term "Opium Lounge",' answered Scarlet. 'But, essentially, yes. I deal in relaxation and contemplation nowadays, as opposed to death and destruction. I find it more soothing to the soul. More fulfilling. And to what do I owe the pleasure of your beautiful self?'

Garrett laughed without humor. 'Death and destruction, I'm afraid, Scarlet.'

The tall man opened the door to a room and walked in. The rest followed to find themselves in an office.

Unlike the rest of the house, it was clean and almost aggressively modern. All stark lines and lightwood furniture and curved stainless steel lamps. Up market IKEA blended with seventies science fiction.

Scarlet gestured towards a semicircle of cream wingback chairs. 'Sit. May I offer you some tea, coffee. Something stronger?'

Garrett shook his head. 'We just had breakfast,' he said. 'Thank you.'

'Tell uncle Scarlet how he can help you. Why are you here?'

Garrett told their story, in detail and leaving nothing out. He finished the story with a request for a safe house and some weaponry.

'A fine tale of derring-do and heroic acts,' responded Scarlet. 'But pray tell, why should Scarlet help?'

'I can pay,' answered Garrett.

Scarlet waved his fish-white hand in the air. 'Pooh and double pooh. I have little need for more money, although there will be a need to cover expenses at very least'

Garrett took a deep breath. 'I can owe you a favor.'

Scarlet smiled, his blindingly white teeth almost negating the need for extra lighting in the room. 'Deal,' he said. 'A large favor.'

'A medium sized favor,' countered Garrett.

Scarlet shook his head. 'No, Scarlet thinks not. Your lives are in danger. I am helping to save them. You, therefore, owe me a life.'

Garrett nodded reluctantly.

The tall man spat into his right hand and proffered it to Garrett who shook it.

'Deal?'

'Deal,' agreed Garrett.

Scarlett opened a drawer on his desk and pulled out a bunch of house keys. He threw them to Garrett.

'The address is written on the tag,' he said. 'It's a house in Fulham. Nice quiet street, very posh.'

He walked over to a filing cabinet and opened the bottom drawer and took out a package. 'Here are two sets of fake license plates. I suggest that you change the plates on your car in case someone is tracking you already.'

Garrett took the plates and nodded his thanks.

'Now, weapons. What are you looking for?'

'Something with firepower, concealable and preferably suppressed,' requested Garrett.

Scarlet nodded. 'I can probably supply something adequate. But before I do, I must warn you, as a rule I no longer deal in arms. Since 9/11 the whole weapons thing has become remarkably tedious, what with the

Americans getting involved. The last thing that I want is to inadvertently sell some hardware to a terrorist and end up in that awful Guantanamo.'

Scarlet went to the filing cabinet once again but this time he pushed it to one side, exposing a lighter concealed panel in the wall. He banged the flat of his hand on the panel and it slid to one side exposing a row of gun-metal gray shelves.

The shelves were on runners and the tall man pulled one open and removed a weapon from it. He handed it to Garrett.

Garrett took it and then he laughed. 'Are you serious?'

Scarlet nodded. 'Deadly. It ticks all of the boxes. High rate of fire, silenced and concealable.'

'It's a relic,' answered Garrett. 'It must be over fifty years old.'

'Sixty-four, actually. But only been test fired once. I can let you have two with six magazines and three hundred rounds of ammunition.'

'What is it?' asked Petrus.

'It's a World War two era Sten gun with a silencer,' said Garrett. 'Come on, Scarlet, I'm looking for a Heckler & Koch, or a Calico. Something that rocks, not a piece of Stone Age crap.'

'Be careful, Garrett. You begin to offend. As I have said, the weapon is adequate. If you would prefer, you could simply fuck off. Go and purchase a set of kitchen knives instead. It fires a 9mm round at a rate of over five hundred a minute. If you keep it clean it won't jam, and the suppressor system is quite remarkable.'

'We'll take them,' said Petrus. 'And thank you very much, mister Scarlet.'

'Yes,' added Garrett. 'Sorry, Scarlet. It was simply a bit of a shock. Better than crossbows though. Thanks. What do I owe you, financially speaking?'

'Two thousand a week for the house and three grand for the weapons and ammo.'

'I thought that you didn't need the money,' said Garrett. 'Five grand seems a little steep.'

'You are buying peace of mind, my friend,' argued Scarlet. 'However, if it's too rich for your blood you can always refer back to my previous advice.'

'What, you mean, fuck off?'

'The very same.'

Garrett laughed, pulled a wad of cash from his pocket and counted out a sheaf. 'Here, seven grand. Two weeks rent.'

Scarlet took the money and threw it casually onto the desk without counting it.

Then he pulled out the second Sten gun, the magazines and the boxes of ammunition. Petrus took it all and started to load it into his tog bag.

While he was doing so, Scarlet rifled through another one of his desk drawers and then came out with a gold chain. On the end was a small cross. He walked over to Lindsey.

'Here we go, princess,' he said. 'A gift from your uncle Scarlet.'

Lindsey glanced at Garrett who gave her a subtle nod.

'Thank you very much,' she responded.

Scarlet dropped the jewelry over Lindsey's head. It was a beautifully crafted piece of work. A plaited chain consisting of white, yellow and red gold, and a cross one inch by half an inch. In the middle of the cross a small ruby twinkled like the eye of Satan.

Scarlet stroked Lindsey's hair and then stood back. She suppressed a shudder and, instead, forced a small smile.

'Beautiful,' he whispered. 'Take care of her, Garrett. Let no harm befall her.'

'I will do my best,' said Garrett.

'And I am sure that will suffice,' responded Scarlet. 'Now, if you gentlemen, and lady, don't mind. I'd rather that you left via the back entrance. Don't want you disturbing my clients any more than you already have. Here, follow me.'

Scarlet led the way down the corridor and showed them out the back of the house, saying his goodbyes as he did.

'That is one seriously creepy old dude,' said Lindsey. 'Nice necklace though.'

'It used to be his daughter's,' said Garrett. 'I actually can't believe that he gave it to you, it was one of his most prized possessions.'

'Where's his daughter now?'

'Dead,' replied Garrett. 'I met Scarlet, actual name, Pierre Du Pont, in the Belgium Congo many years back. I was fighting for Laurent-Désiré Kabila. President Mobutu was supporting the genocide in Rwanda where they had just killed at least eight hundred thousand ethnic Tutsis and moderate Hutus. We were struggling to depose him.

The country was up in flames, towns under siege, roving bands of well-armed bandits. A complete nightmare. He ran a large car dealership in Kinshasa, the county's capital.

'But he lived outside of the town, large colonial style house, servants, a French wife and a beautiful young daughter, Cinderella.'

'What, like the Disney princess?' asked Lindsey. 'Poor girl.'

'Whatever,' said Garrett. 'To cut a long story short, we were on patrol one day, saw smoke and went to investigate. Found Scarlet's house. It was under attack by a group of bandits.

'We drove them off but by the time that we did, Scarlet's wife and daughter had been killed. He lost it. From that day on he was a changed man. He simply left everything that he had and joined up with us. Fought alongside him for almost a year. He was a killing machine, absolutely unstoppable. Frightening.

'Anyhow, after that year we went our separate ways. Got back in contact a few years ago. He's completely insane, but a good friend.'

Lindsey looked closely at the cross that Scarlet had given her. 'That's sad,' she said.

'It is what it is,' said Garrett. 'It is what it is.'

There are almost half a million CCTV cameras in London. One per every twelve people.

Commander Hastings was burning the midnight oil in his office, going over all of the CCTV footage around Lindsey's house at the time that the two men had broken in and assaulted his sergeant.

It didn't take long and he got a hit. But the light was bad and it was right at the edge of the camera's useful distance. He could make out the Land Rover and a partial number plate.

He saw an African man with close cropped hair and a Caucasian male with long dark hair. They were around six feet tall.

He forwarded the images to Debra and she forwarded it to a secure email address that belonged to The Custodians.

It wasn't much but it was a start.

The net had been cast and was trawling the seas that constituted the heaving sprawl of London.

Now it was only a matter of time.

CHAPTER SEVENTEEN

Less than ten years ago The Custodian Group had consisted of three members. And their offices were situated in a rundown hovel in Tower Hamlets. Opposite the chip shop and above an Indian takeaway. Britain's two favorite foods.

Now their offices were in Canada Square, Canary wharf. Fifty floors above London and situated amongst bankers and financial institutions. Their turnover was in the millions a year.

A far cry from the old days.

The Custodian Group employed over sixty people. Mainly ex Israeli MOSSAD, and ex South African BOSS members.

The outfit was run by a man known to all as The Curator. A 65-year-old ex-Rhodesian. Tall, bluff and avuncular, with long gray hair that curled over his collar, and a large moustache. Blue eyes that twinkled in the light and a bulky nose that tended towards the redder end of the spectrum, hinting at a surfeit of alcohol and rich foods.

A Father Christmas exterior that totally belied the stainless-steel sociopath that lurked beneath. The

Curator, actual name, Nigel Taylor, no longer did any of the actual wet work. He limited himself to strictly managerial tasks, hiring, firing and planning.

But, back in the day, when he had still been in the field, he was known to all by the nickname of The Happy Butcher, due to his smile and appearance. Sometimes they simply called him Happy and he encouraged the nickname amongst his partners, particularly the Watchmen.

He was both feared and respected by all who came into contact with him.

Out of the sixty employees, only twenty-four were actual wet-work operatives or Watchmen, as they were designated. Twenty-two men and two women.

The rest were admin and research staff, designated as Attendants.

The Curator had spent the last ten minutes on the burner phone to Debra Haddock and had consequently called a meeting with his 2IC who was also the senior Attendant. Together, the two of them had decided on the team that they considered best for the task.

Three senior Watchmen. Hard men, solid and dependable.

An Israeli, Moshe Malkovitz, five ten, wiry muscle stretched across a spare frame, cropped black hair and dark, lizard-like eyes that never blinked.

Two South Africans. Eugene Visser. six feet two inches tall, massive barrel chest and thick neck. Cauliflower ears, courtesy of rugby, and small piggy eyes that glittered with venom. He sported a massive chip on his shoulder and was racist in a way that only the most paranoid and fearful can be.

And Kobus Van Staden, ex parabat, mercenary. Six foot five with a ragged black beard, short hair and a badly broken nose. Small scar on his upper lip that pulled it into a constant sneer. But, unlike the other two team members, when he smiled his face could light up a room. The massive Afrikaner went by the incongruous nickname of Daisy and, when not smiling, he ran at a constant seven or eight on the anger scale, so even the slightest of inconsequentialities could rev him up to a full ten. Hands as big as shovels and faster than shit out of a goose, he was a man not to be trifled with.

Happy sat at the head of the boardroom table. The three Watchmen sat at the sides, the two Afrikaners together and the Israeli opposite.

'Right, Watchmen,' said Happy 'We have received a new wet work contract. Two men. One black, one white, both considered to be extremely dangerous. Both armed. That is why we have chosen you three, the A team, as it were.

At the moment we have no real info to go on; however, we have help with this one. We will be getting police intelligence on an ad hoc basis as and when the whereabouts of the marks are known. So, tool up, hand guns, silenced. Shouldn't need more than that. Sit back and wait. That will be all.'

The Watchmen nodded and left the boardroom. They didn't talk to each other.

Malkovitz and Visser went to their small offices. Daisy Van Staden decided to visit the canteen. He ordered two large rump steaks, French fries and onion rings and Bunn flask of black coffee. No vegetables. He covered the contents of the plate in ketchup.

The he ate silently, chewing methodically and taking a swig of the black coffee with each mouthful.

After he had eaten, he went to the balcony and lit himself a cigarette. Camel plain. A strong Turkish tobacco blend. The countywide ban on smoking at work was completely ignored at the offices of The Custodian Group. The very idea of banning a group of hired killers from their social drug of choice simply beggared belief. Pretty much all of them smoked, particularly The Watchmen. If you didn't smoke it was a simple case of FIFO – Fit In Or Fuck Off.

Daisy stared out across the Thames. Some people loved the view of the river and the backdrop of London. Van Staden merely saw a place full of people. He was a man who had spent most of his formative life in the bush, either playing as a child, camping as an adolescent or waging war as a young adult. But he had eschewed the bush for an easier life in the city. The life of a city-based assassin boasted less terror, less hardships and a shithouse full of more money. Long gone were his days of patrolling through the jungles carrying a machine gun and praying that the next step would find grass or earth, as opposed to the detonator of an anti-personal mine.

Out of many close compatriots from those days, he was one of a small handful left alive. And that was because, like the other survivors, he had a sixth sense. An inbuilt alarm that seemed to be capable of sniffing out trouble. A sort of mental danger radar. It had saved his life on many a patrol. A feeling of uncomfortableness. A low-grade fear that nagged at the back of the mind like a toothache. A far away fire alarm on the very edge of hearing.

He was feeling it now, and he had no idea why.

He drew deeply on his cigarette and thought. It was probably nothing. Perhaps he had simply been doing this job for too long. He had seen it happen before. Fear builds up like barnacles on a ship, below the waterline where no one can see them. But they slow the ship down. They impede it. Rob it of its speed and maneuverability.

And then one day, during a crisis, the ship needs to call on its speed. Its power. Its inherent maneuverability.

But instead, it flounders because of the barnacles. It sinks.

Fear.

It can kill.

Daisy lit another cigarette and forced himself to relax.

'Calm down,' he whispered to himself. 'There is nothing out there that you need be afraid of.'

Nothing.

CHAPTER EIGHTEEN

Debra Haddock strode into the workshop and stared at Bradley Parker.

The minister was flanked by two wiry SAS soldiers, their eyes a reflection of their brutal competence, and their stances indicative of their innate superiority.

Professor Parker glanced up. His eyes were rimmed with dark circles, the left one twitched slightly. Tiny involuntary movements. He smelt unwashed. Sour.

His deep exhaustion was obvious.

Debra wrinkled her nose at the odor. 'Parker,' she said. 'You are a disappointment to us. A huge disappointment.'

The professor looked up from his work. 'This is not Lego, Debra,' he said. 'This literally is nuclear physics. If you wanted to build tinker toys you should have kidnapped a toddler to do it. It takes time.'

'I concede the point, professor, but surely not this much time. I suspect that you may be deliberately dragging your feet.'

Parker threw down his micrometer and folded his arms across his chest like a sulky adolescent. 'Well, you do it then,' he huffed.

'Professor,' countered the minister. 'Do I need to remind you that we have your daughter in captivity?'

'Do you? So you say? For all I know you could have already killed her. I demand to talk to her. I swear – not one more stitch of work will I do until I have spoken to my daughter.'

Haddock looked at one of the soldiers and nodded her head.

The man stepped forward and punched the professor in the stomach. Parker fell to the floor with a grunt and the soldier followed up with a kick to his ribs. Then he picked the professor up by his collar and stood him in front of Debra Haddock.

The professor struggled to regain his breath and, when he did, he shouted at the minister. 'Do what you will, you rancid hag. But not one more thing will you get out of me. I want to hear from my daughter.'

The soldier swung a sharp left-hand jab at Parker's face and the professor's nose broke with a dull crunch. Blood gushed down his face and tears of pain sprung from his eyes as he fell to the ground again.

'Fuck you, you devil woman,' he grunted. 'Beat me if you will. Beat me until I can't do your vile insane work. I don't care. But I guarantee you, on all that is logical in this world, no message from my daughter - no more work. So fuck you, you psychotic bitch.'

Haddock stared at him for a while and then stormed from the room followed by one of the soldiers, the other staying inside with the beaten professor.

Outside in the corridor she stopped for a moment and thought. Finally, she turned to the soldier. 'You, sergeant Robbie.'

'It's sergeant Robhurst, ma'am.'

'Whatever, look, I don't know if colonel Peterson has kept you in the loop, but your moronic compatriots have managed to lose the professor's daughter. There's no way that she can phone daddy, as her whereabouts are currently unknown. So, I need you to find a girl of similar age and race. Twelve, fair skin, about five feet one inch.'

The sergeant raised an eyebrow. 'With all respect ma'am, there's no way that we could pass her off as his daughter. I mean, the man isn't grotesquely stupid, quite the contrary.'

Haddock looked at the SAS soldier with contempt. 'We are not going to try to pass her off as his daughter sergeant Robsdon,' she snapped.

'Robhurst, ma'am.'

'Jesus Christ, nobody fucking cares, sergeant. Anyhow, I want you to find a girl that fits the bill, do it as soon as. And when you find her, remove her right index finger and bring it to me.'

Robhurst did a double take. 'Her finger, ma'am?'

'Yes sergeant, her finger. What's the problem, are you deaf as well as slow witted?'

The sergeant stared at the minister for a few seconds. Then Debra leaned closer to the soldier. 'Listen, sergeant Robhurst,' she said, her voice low and soft. Almost intimate. 'You know what is riding on this. Your country needs you. The United Kingdom is relying on you, on your strength of character. Can we rely on you?'

Robhurst nodded. 'Yes, ma'am. You well know that I place my country above all. I will not let you down. Her finger. Understood. What should I do with the girl after that?'

Haddock shrugged. 'I only need the finger, sergeant; the rest is superfluous to our needs. Dispose of it as you will.'

The soldier saluted her 'Ma'am.'

Debra patted his cheek. 'Thank you, sergeant Robhurst,' she said. 'I can tell that you and I will work well together. I see a great future for you in the new order. Stick with me and you will not regret it.'

Then she turned and left, taking out her cell and dialing as she did. 'Commander, give me some good news. Have you tracked them down? Oh, well done Jarvis. Great work, forward the video footage to me and I shall inform the Custodians at once.'

As she left the building, the SAS sergeant shook his head. 'Fuck me,' he said to himself. 'That is one serious fucking woman. When she's in charge then we can finally kick those jihadist's asses for good.'

And he grinned to himself, looking forward to some payback for the friends that he had lost in both Iraq and Afghanistan.

CHAPTER NINETEEN

The Happy Butcher received the CCTV footage from Debra via Commander Hastings. Haddock and sent for the three Watchmen so they could view it with him.

They were using the small boardroom for the viewing and Happy's Apple lap top sat on the table, connected wirelessly to a seventy-two-inch LED TV screen.

The Curator waited until all three of the Watchmen were seated.

'Gentlemen,' he started. 'We have some CCTV footage of our targets. I warn you that it's a little grainy and, ultimately, it's not much to go on, but it's a start. Our principle has sent it so that we are kept in the loop and all subsequent info will be imparted on a similar basis.'

Happy turned on the laptop and the huge TV lit up...we see a typical upper middle class London residential road. A mix of Victorian and Georgian housing. White plaster and red face-brick. Cast iron railings, mature trees line the sidewalks. Bux hedges.

A Land Rover drives slowly down the road and then pulls in to park. Two men climb out. One is black, the other white. It looks as though there may be a third person on the back seat. Small. A woman., maybe a child. The light is bad so it is hard to see properly.

The men set off down the road, they move like athletes, walking on the balls of their feet. But unlike athletes, their heads are constantly moving, scanning from side to side.

Like predators.

The white man stops just before they take a right turn into someone's back yard. He revolves slowly, taking in the entire street. Giving the area a last once over.

Daisy drew in a sharp breath. 'Wait,' he said. 'Can you rewind that?'

Happy did so without questioning.

'Pause it.'

The image pauses. The man is staring almost directly into the CCTV camera.

'Is there any way that you can zoom in? asked Daisy.

'There is,' answered Happy. 'But it will blur the image even more.'

'Please try.'

Happy fiddled with his lap top and the image on the TV grew larger, centered on the man's face.

'I don't fucking believe it,' gasped Daisy. 'No way, it can't be.'

'Can't be what?' asked Happy.

Daisy shuddered. 'It is Popobawa. It is…The Beast.'

All three men turned to look at Daisy.

As always, they saw a huge man, scarred face, large broken nose, pale blue eyes that seemed always to look through you. The proverbial thousand-yard stare. But for the first time since any of them have known him they saw something else…they saw a man who was afraid. And he was not even attempting to hide the fact.

Daisy started to talk; his voice quiet, remote. Dead. Almost as if he was reading from a list.

'Back in the day, after my time in the South African bush war, I became a mercenary. Stuck to Africa. I knew the place, spoke a few of the languages and there were, actually still are, plenty of wars to fight. Long story short, I was hired by an American outfit that was working for president Kabbah of Sierra Leone. Ended up being seconded to a small reaction force group. A sort of roving Special Forces. Shit happened; we were sent to sort it out.'

The big man lit a cigarette, inhaled and thought for a bit. No one rushed him. They had all been there; they knew that the retelling of certain things could be difficult. Incidents that the mind kept filed away. Hidden from view. Sealed up in order to keep the thin veneer of sanity that any long-term combat soldier lives under.

'Look,' Daisy continued. 'I'm not going to go into the whole thing, let's just say, things got seriously out of hand very quickly. Our captain,' Daisy pointed at the screen. 'His name was…is, Garrett. Garrett, something Scottish. Can't remember, actually, I'm not even sure if I ever really knew. Just called him Captain, or Boss.

'Anyhow, we drove into a village one day, see all these kids, little fuckers. As innocent as the day that they were born, maybe six, seven years old…some as young as four. Some are alive. Some dead. Many dying. The rebels had taken them and,' he drew on his cigarette again and shook his head as if he still couldn't believe it. 'They had taken them and chopped their fucking hands off. All of them. Left a little pile of kiddie's hands in the middle of the village.' Tears started to glaze the big man's eyes over. 'I swear to you, that was the saddest, most pathetic thing that I've ever seen. That little pile of hands.'

Daisy shook his head like a dog. 'Garrett went mad. I mean…something inside him snapped…that thing, whatever it is, it's what keeps you human. It broke. We went after the people that did that to the kids. We chased them for days. He pushed us harder than I've ever been pushed in my life. Beyond exhaustion. No rest, no sleep.

'When we found them, he made us chop off their hands and their feet. But he kept them alive. Said that they didn't deserve to die. He made the villagers swear that they would keep those men alive, crawling on the earth like worms. But it didn't end there. He kept us going…until, eventually there was no one left to hunt.'

Daisy shuddered. 'Man...he used to howl when he fought. Like a fucking animal. Like a beast. The locals called him Popobawa...The Demon. Others...The Beast.

'Then one day – he left. We don't know where he went. Or why. He just left us in that shithole of a country. Eventually we fought our way to the border. A few years later I joined this mob.

'Never thought that I'd see that face again.'

Daisy looked at the butt of his cigarette, a scowl on his face.

Then he spoke again. 'Happy.'

'Yes.'

'We'll need more men. Three of us aren't enough. I swear to you.'

Happy nodded. He knew Daisy Van Staden well enough to know the huge Afrikaner was being very serious. He also knew he didn't exaggerate, in fact, normally quite the opposite.

'How many then, Daisy?' he asked.

Van Staden shook his head. He looked like a child that had just been woken up from a nightmare.

'We don't have enough,' he whispered.

CHAPTER TWENTY

Debra entered the lab with sergeant Robhurst. Professor Parker was asleep in his chair, his face lying on his work bench, his hair a grease encrusted tangle and his clothes now almost brittle with dirt and sweat. His captors allowed him to leave the lab twice a day for bathroom breaks only. The rest of the time they drove him mercilessly.

But he still was running days behind their expected schedule.

'Get him up,' commanded Debra. 'And hold his arms.'

The sergeant complied, dragging the professor upright and grasping his shoulders.

Debra Haddock stood close to Parker and, when she was sure that the man was fully awake, she took a cloth wrapped object from her purse, unrolled it and held it in front of Bradley Parker's face.

It was the right-hand forefinger from a child.

'Do you see what your attitude has led to?' asked Debra, her voice strident. Harsh. 'Now do you see what you have done to your daughter?'

Bradley stared at the dismembered finger for a few seconds, his face expressionless and his eyes blank as he tried to take in the enormity of what Debra was showing him.

And then his expression changed to one of absolute horror.

He snarled like an animal and lunged forward with such strength that sergeant Robhurst lost grip. As he broke free, he swung an awkward punch at the minister.

It was an untrained blow, thrown by a peaceable man. But it was powered by a vast well of hatred.

The blow landed squarely on Debra's nose with a satisfying crunch as the cartilage split and the delicate bones broke. Blood gushed from the wound and the minister fell to the floor with a pig-like squeal of agony.

But the professor wasn't finished. He started screaming incoherently, his voice a guttural, broken cacophony. And at the same time, he launched a massive soccer-kick into the minister's ribs. Again, he was rewarded with the crunch of bone breaking as Debra's right hand false-rib snapped under the assault.

Bradley pulled his foot back, readying himself for another kick but before he could, sergeant Robhurst rabbit-punched him in the back of his head and he fell to the floor, unconscious.

Robhurst grabbed a pile of paper towels from the work bench and knelt next to the prostrate form of the minister. 'Ma'am, are you alright?' he asked as he handed her the paper towels so that she could staunch the flow of blood coming from her broken nose.

'No I am not,' yelled Debra. 'What the hell? How did that happen?'

'I'm sorry, ma'am,' answered Robhurst. 'The strength that he pulled away with, it took me by surprise. I think that we need to get you to a doctor, ma'am.'

'I'm fine,' said Debra. 'Where's the finger?' she started scrabbling on the floor. 'The finger, sergeant.'

Robhurst saw the severed digit on the floor under the work bench. He retrieved it and handed it to the minister.

'I don't want it,' she snapped. 'We need to keep it as a reminder. Keep him motivated. Put it in the fridge or something.'

Debra's cell stated to ring. She glanced at the screen.

'For fuck's sake,' she cursed. 'I'm going to have to take this. You, sergeant, wake this prick up and get him working. Do it.' She raised the phone to her ear. 'Yes….oh, excellent. At least something is going right. No, I'm fine. Blocked nose is all. Thank you for the information, commander. I wonder if you could text me the address and then I can forward the info to the Custodians. Thank you.'

The Happy Butcher smiled to himself. The Elephant and Castle. Debra Haddock had supplied him with an address and given the go ahead. His three targets were last seen entering a large Victorian house and, if it was up to Happy, they would not be exiting it.

Taking Daisy's advice into account, Happy had put together a six man kill team. He had included Malkovitz and Visser in the team but had left out Daisy. It wasn't that he didn't trust the big man to do his job, it was simply that the look of undisguised fear on his face had been unsettling to say the least. Happy thought it better to simply leave the big man on the sidelines for a while until he had recovered.

***

Scarlet frowned in annoyance. Someone was hammering aggressively on his front door. As insistent as a drunken sailor at a whore house.

He glanced at his watch and frowned. It couldn't be Garrett again, he had everything that he needed, and he had left over an hour ago.

The rooms were not fully booked at the moment but Scarlet was not expecting any more clients, and his establishment wasn't the sort of place that encouraged walk-in clientele. He looked at the CCTV screen and saw a man dressed in a black tight t-shirt, long black combat trousers and desert boots.

Scarlet manipulated the camera using the keypad next to the screen, lifting it up and getting as wide a shot as possible. Just visible at the edge of the screen he could see at least another three men. They were dressed in a similar fashion, but they were carrying weapons.

Skorpion sub machine guns, chambered for .32 ACP rounds. Vicious little weapons designed for a pray and spray as opposed to accurate work. They were obviously prepared for extremely wet work.

Scarlet smiled. It was obvious why they were there. One thing about Garrett, thought Scarlet to himself, he keeps one's life interesting. The opium dealer shook his head, annoyed with himself. He should have been more prepared - ever since he had known the soldier, Garrett had attracted trouble, like a pile of shit attracts flies.

Scarlet thought that it had something to do with the soldier's overblown sense of right and wrong. He felt he was fated to solve the wrongs of the world and, as a result, he spent the majority of his life being disappointed.

He adjusted the camera again zooming in slightly and bringing into focus a man with a pistol grip shotgun, on the end of the barrel was a serrated extension, specifically for ballistic breaching. The man rammed the end against the top hinges and pulled the trigger. There was a solid thump and then he moved to the bottom hinge and repeated the process, blowing the door off its hinges.

Before the door hit the floor Scarlet was already pushing the filing cabinet aside and opening his gun shelves. He pulled out a shelf and grabbed a Mossberg high-capacity pump action shotgun loaded with ten rounds of 12-gauge buckshot.

He heard the men run into the building, combat boots hammering on the carpeted wooden floors. He peeked around the corner, stealing a quick glance.

There are at least six of them.

Two went into the first opium room, there were clients there, lounging on silk cushions, embalmed with shadow and sedated by a haze of opium fumes.

The prolonged burp of the silenced Skorpions brought an abrupt end to life, like pair of insane typewriters hammering a row of periods onto a page. Life's full stops.

The killers ran out of the room, changing their magazines as they did so.

'Clear,' shouted the one. 'They're not there.'

They ran into the next room, kicking the door open as they did. The same ripping sound of death stuttered from the room as they murdered the occupants.

It was now utterly obvious the kill team were looking for Garrett and his friend. And the little girl.

'Screw them,' said Scarlet to himself. 'Coming in here and treating me with such disrespect. Killing my clients, trying to kill my friends. Time to die.'

The tall man stepped out into the corridor and slammed off eight rounds, filling the air with lead shot. Each double O shell contains 9 lead balls of shot. Scarlet moved the shotgun from left to right racking and firing as fast as he could, filling the corridor with over seventy high velocity lead slugs. Three of the intruders were literally torn to shreds as the lead smashed into them.

The noise was absolutely deafening.

The two other men came out of a client room and opened fire at him.

Scarlet ducked down and returned fire, pumping the shotgun twice, shouting out his anger and defiance and rage, then dropping the empty weapon as he ran at them.

A bullet hit him in the center of his torso, knocking the wind out of him as his sternum cracked and the air was driven from his lungs. He struggled to take a shuddering breath. It felt like someone had struck him in the chest with a burning sledge hammer.

But he kept running forward, barreling into the one assassin, hitting him like a Mack truck. Almost three hundred pounds of pissed off.

Scarlet flicked out his right arm and, like magic, a long slim stiletto blade appeared in his hand. He rammed it into the attacker's solar plexus, driving it upward into his heart.

Behind him the other man fired point blank into the tall man's back. Scarlet felt his ribs shatter as the small, high velocity rounds hammered into him. He spun and slashed out with the stiletto; it sliced through the man's throat with ease, but as it hit the murderer's neck vertebrae, the thin blade snapped off.

Blood squirted out, painting the walls in deep red blood, like the devil's fire extinguisher.

'And that's why they call me Scarlet,' shouted the tall man with a smile.

A final attacker ran out of the last client room and sprayed the corridor with bullets as he did so. Two of the rounds struck Scarlet in the stomach, tearing flesh and severing internal organs.

He bellowed like a gut shot buffalo and charged again. The man frantically tried to change his magazine for a fresh one but Scarlet was on him before he could. Two massive, ham sized hands, one ochre, one corpse white wrapped around the man's neck and he squeezed.

The assassin slapped and punched at Scarlet but it was like fighting against a glacier. Slow and inexorable. Bones ground together, cartilage popped as it was crushed and, finally, nerves were severed.

The man did an obscene little jig and then went still.

Scarlet dropped the body to the floor.

A tsunami of pain crashed over him and he fell to his knees. Then he slowly crawled into a client room. There were two dead people in there.

'What a waste,' he said to no one in particular. 'Why kill everyone?' He picked up a full Opium pipe and lay down on a large silk pillow. Then he held the pipe over a small lit oil lamp, waited for it to heat through and dragged in a lungful. It made him cough and pain tore through him. He forced himself to take another draw. This time it was easier.

After the third hit most of the pain had receded to manageable level.

As the opium relaxed him, he remained aware of the pain while, at the same time, it no longer bothered him.

With a shock he realized he had better warn Garrett some seriously heavy hitters were looking for him. He struggled to get his cell phone out but, by the time he had, he realized he didn't have his number. In fact, he never had.

Then Scarlet started to laugh to himself, the Opium lifting his spirits and enhancing his sense of humor to the point that all was amusing.

'Let them find Garrett,' he chuckled. 'They'll come; he'll kill them. Then he'll track down whoever sent the assassins and he'll kill them too. And then he will kill anyone one else that had anything to do with it. I will be avenged, you stupid mother fuckers.'

The tall man laughed again. It was the classic case of the hunters becoming the hunted.

He took another hit on the pipe and closed his eyes.

And far, far away he heard a voice calling. Welcoming him.

'I gave your cross away, my darling,' he whispered to the voice.

It called him again and he reached out towards it.

Scarlet died with a smile on his face.

CHAPTER TWENTY-TWO

Happy lit a cigar; it took him longer than usual because he kept fumbling, his fingers refusing to perform the minor fine motor skills necessary for the task.

If he was being completely honest with himself, he would admit that he was actually in a mild state of shock. But it would not do to admit such a weakness.

'But what the hell?' he asked himself. 'How could that have just happened?'

When he hadn't received a sitrep from the kill team he sent to the Elephant and Castle, he sent another back up team to report on the situation.

They had found a massacre. And from what they told him it had been one guy who had taken them all out. Dead bodies everywhere, stoners full of holes, his men torn to shreds from shotgun fire, throats cut, one man with his head almost ripped off and a dead gangster in a purple suit with a smile on his face.

'What the hell?' he questioned again, his bafflement robbing him of his usual verbal eloquence.

And the worst of it was that none of the dead were the target people. Where were they?

He picked up his phone and rang Debra.

Twenty miles away, sitting in an office with Colonel Grant Peterson, Debra Haddock answered and listened to the Curator without interrupting. However, her expression was enough to judge her feelings.

'Mister Taylor, or Curator or Happy or whatever you call yourself,' she hissed into the phone. 'You sort this goat-fuck of a mission out, or I promise that your group will receive no more work from this government or any other. Clean up this mess. Do I make myself clear?'

She disconnected and threw the phone down on the table top.

'What's the problem?' asked colonel Peterson.

'What isn't the problem?' snapped Haddock. 'I seem to be surrounded by fools and idiots. The Custodians couldn't organize a killing in an abattoir. Commander Hastings is late, as usual, and Professor Parker is definitely dragging his feet.'

'It will all come right, Debra,' said Peterson.

The minister stood up and began to pace around the room. 'It had better, Grant. I've spent years setting this up. And for those same years I have had to watch my country slowly erode as the left eats away at its very fabric. The heart of our proud nation is being flooded and drowned by a flood of foreigners and Islamic radicals.

'Our pathetic, pink-politicians are more worried about political correctness than they are about waging a war on Islam and its followers. For God's sake,' she continued. 'Most of them won't even admit that we are at war. And if we can't name our enemy, how can we ever beat him?'

'Preaching to the converted, Debra,' responded the colonel. 'You well know that Jarvis and I are in full agreement. I'm an officer in an army that is now little more than a minor ally to the Americans. We no longer have a navy to speak of, our fighter jet capability is a joke and now we can't even get funding for the submarine program. Even our boys on the ground have substandard equipment, crappy body armor, shoddy boots and the world's worst communication systems. I fear that we have finally reached the stage where we no longer have an actual working defense force.'

'That will all change,' said Haddock. 'I know Jarvis and you were initially appalled at my plan, but now you see it is all we can do. Thousands of good British people will die, but they will do so as true martyrs. True heroes.

'Because, when we detonate that nuclear bomb on the outskirts of Birmingham and pin the blame on Isil, there will be no turning back. The ire of the British people will ensure that we finally react in the way that we should have from the very beginning. Britain, Europe, America. The rest of the Christian world will fall on the Muslims like the wrath of God. We will exterminate their evil from the face of the earth. People will be left with no other choice after such a terrible atrocity.'

And then the Empire will need a new leader, thought minister Haddock to herself. A strong leader. A new Iron Lady. Like Thatcher but harder, stricter. Stronger.

At that moment commander Hastings burst into the room.

'Good afternoon, all,' he blurted. 'Sorry that I'm late, but good news. I have reacquired the targets. I have the address where they are staying.'

Haddock smiled, her features a study in vulpine pleasure. 'Good work,' she said. 'Give it to me.'

CHAPTER TWENTY-THREE

The Watchmen came for Garrett and Petrus and Lindsey at midnight.

There were six of them. They picked the door and slid into the house on rubber soled feet, dressed in black.

All six carried the silenced Skorpion .32 sub machine guns favored by the Custodian Group.

Three stayed at the bottom of the stairs and three crept up, keeping their feet on the outside of the stair boards to ensure that they made no sound. Death approached silently as they glided down the corridor and then stopped, one outside each occupied room.

One man held his hand up and ticked off the timing on his fingers.

One, two, three – all reached for the door handles and turned them slowly, easing the doors open with glacial speed.

They stepped into the rooms.

The first man raised his machine-pistol, aimed at the still mound on the bed.

And then the darkness exploded into life. There was the flash of a machete and the Watchman's hand literally leapt from his arm in a welter of blood, the hand and weapon landing noiselessly on the bed. Then the massive blade reversed in the air and flicked back slashing through the assassin's neck.

The body slumped silently to the carpet.

Garrett moved again, whispering as he did so. 'Lindsey, stay in the closet, one minute.'

He ghosted through the door and, as he did so, he heard the sound of a body sliding down the wall in the next room.

Petrus stepped out, his assegai dark with a deep red coating.

The dull burp of a silenced sub machine gun thudded from the room that Lindsey was meant to be in. Petrus stepped into the bedroom and slammed his assegai through the shooter's shoulder blades. A foot of steel magically appeared out of the man's chest. Then Petrus twisted the blade savagely before he pulled it out, accompanied by a grotesque wet sucking sound.

The man sank to the floor.

Both Garrett and Petrus unslung their Sten guns and Garrett led the way out into the corridor.

There were three men downstairs, two at the foot of the staircase and one standing at the door.

Garrett aimed and pulled the trigger, a one and a half second burst that burned off ten rounds. The Sten was everything that Scarlet had said and more. Garrett registered the fact that he had better apologize to the old bastard the next time he saw him.

The ancient suppressor let out a bare purring pulse of sound and the 9 mm rounds packed a vicious punch. Both of the men went down in a storm of blood and flesh and chips of wood and pieces of mortar.

The man at the door returned fire but both Garrett and Petrus fired back and a hail of lead hammered the man into the door, killing him before he slid to the tiled floor.

Then silence.

Garrett ran down the steps, checked that the men were all dead and then he quickly scanned the rest of the downstairs.

Petrus called out. 'Princess. It's safe. Come on down.'

The young girl came out of the room and flinched when she saw the bloodied bodies at the bottom of the stairs.

'How did you know that they were coming?' she asked. 'I mean...one second I was asleep, next you woke me and less than a minute later they were here.'

Garrett shrugged. 'We just know. It's what we do. It's a gift. It's why we're still alive. Maybe it's a curse. Let's go, we need to move out right now. First, Petrus, let's pick up some weapons and ammo and whatever else these dudes were carrying.'

The two friends quickly searched the bodies. They took two Skorpions and ten magazines of ammunition.

'Hey, check this out,' said Petrus.

'What?'

The Zulu held up a bulky pair of goggles. 'Some sort of night vision goggles. Should we take them?'

Garrett shook his head. 'You can if you want to. I hate those things. They disconnect you from the environment. Also, they never seem to work when you need them to.'

Petrus shrugged and dropped the offending piece of equipment to the floor.

Then they grabbed their various items of personal kit and ran to the Land Rover, piling in and pulling off immediately.

At the end of the street a big man watched them through a small pair of binoculars, he thumbed his cell phone. It rang and was picked up immediately.

'Hello, Daisy. Is it done?' asked the Curator.

'Negative, Curator. The two men are leaving the house now. They have the girl with them. It looks as if they have terminated the team.'

'Impossible.'

'I did warn you, sir.'

'Fuck sakes. Can you see their number plate?'

'Yes.'

'Give it to me. Don't follow them, they might spot you. Wait until they're gone and then get into the house. See if any of the team are alive.'

'They won't be, sir.'

'Just check, Van Staden, for God's sake', cursed Happy. 'Keep in touch.'

He disconnected and fumbled in his pocket for a cigar. Then he cut it and spent some time lighting it perfectly, turning it round in the flame and drawing gently. He forced himself to concentrate on the simple task, ensuring that he did it without shaking hands.

How can this be happening? He thought to himself. He took a deep drag, but the smoke tasted bitter. Acrid and dirty.

It tasted of defeat.

He had lost over half of his Watchmen.

And he hadn't even managed to scratch the targets.

CHAPTER TWENTY-FOUR

The Land Rover stood on the side of the road in the London suburb of Putney.

'How the hell did they find us?' asked Garrett to no one in particular.

'Maybe Scarlet told them,' suggested Petrus.

'Never,' denied Garrett. 'Trust me on that.'

'CCTV cameras,' said Lindsey. 'There's like half a million of them in London. The average Londoner is caught about three hundred times a day.'

'So what?' asked Garrett. 'To find us they would have to have a platoon of dudes watching them.'

Lindsey shook her head. 'Uh uh. If they know what we look like, then they'll just run their facial recognition programs. They'll find us for sure.'

'What if we wear disguises?' asked Petrus.

'Well, maybe if they're really sophisticated. Or maybe if we all wear burkas, or rubber masks. Even then it also depends how much info that they have on us. Their software can pick up the way that we walk, mannerisms, that sort of stuff.'

Garrett nodded. 'Well, that's cool because we don't want to hide anymore. In fact, it's time to take these assholes out. Look, at the moment we aren't sure how many recourses they have at their disposal, but we've taken out a few of their guys. The thing is, the last lot were definitely not SAS or cops. I've seen their type before. '

'Mercenaries,' said Petrus.

'Yep,' agreed Garrett. 'Hired guns. Pro assassins. Some looked South African. A couple were definitely Israeli. That smack of outside contractors. So, I would guess that means that the boys that we are up against, the original kidnappers, don't have unlimited recourses. They've had to contract work out. That's good, because contactors don't like to lose men.

'Now, at the moment all of the advantages lie with the enemy. They know London better than us, there are undoubtedly more of them than us and they will have better weapons and access to better equipment. But I have a plan.'

'What?' asked Petrus.

'Well, where do we do our best work?'

Petrus laughed. 'In the bush.'

'Exactly.'

'Good one,' laughed Petrus. 'It's simple then, all we have to do is go back to Africa, leave a trail for them to follow, wait for them, ambush them – problems over.'

Garrett grinned. 'You got it.'

Petrus' smile faded. 'Come one, don't be stupid.'

'No,' retorted Garrett. 'I'm serious. Okay, we obviously can't get them back to Africa, but we can get them into an open outdoor environment that suits us over them.'

'Where?'

'Richmond Park.'

Lindsey clapped her hands. 'Brilliant.'

Petrus shrugged. 'That means nothing to me.'

'Well,' said Lindsey. 'Richmond Park is situated in south west London. It covers an area of two thousand acres, has over six hundred deer and is surrounded by a high wall. But they allow access twenty-four hours a day for bicycles and pedestrians.'

'How do you know all of that?' asked Petrus

'Brain the size of a planet,' smirked the young girl.

'Still, it's not Africa,' said Petrus. 'But it's definitely not inner-city London. So, what's the rest of the plan?'

'It's simple,' replied Garrett. 'We head for Richmond Park, look to get there just before sundown. We make sure that we're picked up by CCTV going in - and we wait. They'll come for us.

'We'll need to stash Lindsey somewhere in the park, probably in a tree hide or similar.

'Then we take our pursuers out. Try to keep at least one alive so that we can question him. He'll talk, there's no reason why he shouldn't. He's a gun for hire, not a convert or a patriot, we threaten him and he'll talk. For sure...I know that I would.'

'What's a tree hide?' asked Lindsey.

'Just a hideaway in the tree tops,' answered Garrett. 'It's always a good place to hide. Most people don't look up enough. Even professionals.'

'Great,' said Lindsey. 'You guys are turning me into a monkey fugitive.'

Petrus laughed. 'Better baboon than buried.'

Lindsey looked scared.

'Don't worry, Princess,' said Petrus. 'I won't let anything happen to you; I swear.'

'Right, troops,' said Garrett. 'We've got a day to kill. What do we need? any requests?'

'A few small ones,' Answered Petrus. 'Something in a squad support weapon. A 7.62 belt fed machine gun would do. Twenty claymores, an AKM assault rifle and a few grenades.'

'Sorry,' replied Garrett. 'All we got is the two Stens and those crappy Skorpions and a couple of Walthers.'

'Oh well,' sighed Petrus theatrically. 'That'll do.'

'You've got your spear and your big knife,' added Lindsey sarcastically.

The two men turned to her and smiled. And she had a glimpse of what it would be like to fall into a shark tank with two giant ragged tooth man eaters. She shivered in vicarious fear.

Garrett cranked the starter and drove to a hardware superstore.

As they drove, Lindsey pointed out landmarks to Petrus.

'Look,' she said. 'That's Stamford Bridge, home of Chelsea Football Club. Capacity, forty-one thousand seven hundred and ninety-eight. The club is worth over one point three billion dollars.'

Petrus grunted. 'Don't watch soccer much.'

'Over there, on the horizon,' continued Lindsey like a tour guide. 'You can see the four chimneys of the Battersea Power Station. Built in the 1930's and stopped producing electricity in the early 1980's. Currently being converted into apartments, shops, offices and so on.'

'Fascinating,' sighed Petrus as he watched a tall blond woman cross the road, walking a dog the size of a hamster.

'That was the Thames River that we crossed earlier, of course,' continued his personal tour guide. 'Did you know that two thirds of London's drinking water comes from the Thames? Also, an average of one body a week is retrieved from the river.'

'What are you, some sort of walking encyclopedia?' laughed Petrus.

'I read stuff and I remember it,' answered Lindsey. 'Can't help it.'

'It's cool,' said Petrus. 'Interesting, actually.'

Garrett pulled into the parking lot of the superstore. 'You two wait here, maybe get some grub there,' he pointed at a caravan selling bacon sandwiches, cheeseburgers and sodas. 'I won't be long.'

He came back about forty minutes later.

Petrus thrust a burger at him and he ate it in three massive bites.

Lindsey made mock gagging sounds. 'Yuck, you eat like an animal.'

Garrett grinned. 'Yum,' he said and patted his stomach.

Then he chucked two bags onto the back seat. Lindsey took a look at them. Inside the first one was a reel of fishing line, a bag of six-inch steel nails, duct tape, a long length of strong rope and a large olive-green tarpaulin. In the second bag was a large orange box marked, "Hot Hands x 200 units", and a small blue aerosol spray can.

'What are these?' she asked, holding the box up.

'Disposable hand warmers,' answered Garrett. 'Two hundred of them. They're just little packets of chemicals. They self-activate when you take them out of their wrappers. Stay hot for eight hours.'

'I know that it's cold,' observed Lindsey. 'But why so many?'

'It's in case the mercs bring more of those thermal sights with them. Trust me, I have a plan, I haven't simply developed a fetish for hand warmers.'

Lindsey laughed. 'Okay, I trust you.' Then she held up the blue aerosol can. 'Doggy-go-away,' she read. 'Dog repellent?' She shook her head. 'Actually, don't bother explaining. I'm not even going to go there.' She put the canister back in the bag.

'Now let's drive to Richmond Park,' said Garrett. 'We pick one of the entrances that stay open and we make ourselves visible. Before sundown we go inside and hope that we've been spotted. Lindsey, will the facial recognition thing still recognize us if we wear caps and sunglasses?'

'Yep, it's very sophisticated.'

'Good, I'll make another stop and we'll pick up some baseball caps and some cheap shades, we'll all wear them so it looks as if we've tried to disguise ourselves.'

Petrus shook his head. 'I'm not super happy about this,' he said. 'There are no ways that this can be construed as a sure-fire plan, my friend.

'So, okay – they see that we're at Richmond Park; they assume that we've gone inside in order to escape detection for a while. They come to the park...then what? How do they find us? How do we find them? In fact, why would they even bother?'

'They'll bother,' said Garrett. 'We offed six of them. They'll come for us, however slim the chance. As to how they find us, simple – we scout the place out for a bit and then pick the most obvious place to hide.

'We stash Lindsey somewhere else...then we wait for them to track us down and we take care of them.'

Petrus shrugged. 'Okay then, I suppose that we can't lose anything by trying.'

'It'll work,' said Garrett with more conviction than he felt. 'It'll work.'

And he pulled off into the traffic.

CHAPTER TWENTY-FIVE

Carlton Ambrose had emigrated from Jamaica in the early 1980's. Within a week he had gotten a good job driving a London bus. Double Decker, red and gleaming. Bigger than the house that he had left back in the islands.

But then his girlfriend had left him, and things had gone downhill from there. Social drinking had turned to something more serious and eventually he was both jobless and homeless. So the streets had become his home, and begging and low level grifting his means of income.

And he had seen many things while on the streets of one of the world's most vibrant capitals. He had seen IRA bombs, he had seen 7/7 and the London riots. Always in the background. A watcher from afar.

But this was the first time that he had seen the Angel of Death himself.

Carlton was bundled up in his sleeping bag, an old relic, bulked up using scraps of material he had collected over time. Wrapped in a sheet of black plastic and hidden under a thick bush to protect himself from the elements.

He looked up and standing over him was a living shadow. Over six feet in height. Its eyes were lit by the moon and they were filled with both wisdom and madness. But the madness was controlled, like it had an intimate knowledge of lunacy, yet the actual insanity itself did not affect it.

It was simply something that the shadow lived with. Something that it called on when needed.

And Carlton knew his time had come. It was his time to die. The only thing that puzzled him was the fact that the Angel of Death didn't carry a scythe. Instead, it carried a wicked short spear with a wide razor-sharp blade, the edges of which gleamed in the moonlight like two slivers of a man's soul.

'So,' he said. 'Finally, after all these years, you have come for me.'

The angel shook its head.

'Then what are you doing here?'

'I have come for others,' it said. 'You must stay here. Do not move until morning.'

He nodded. 'I will not move.'

The angel nodded back and started to depart.

Before it left Carlton asked. 'Death. When will you come to take me?'

The Angel smiled. Its mouth was covered but Carlton could see the smile in its eyes.

'No one knows. Not even me. But you will not die before your time,' it said.

And then it disappeared, vanishing into the night.

Carlton Ambrose, formerly of Kingston, Jamaica, and now of no fixed abode, pulled his sleeping bag over his head and lay still. Content that he had escaped Death for a while longer.

Garrett looked up as Petrus arrived 'Did I hear you talking to someone?'

'Yep,' acknowledged the Zulu. 'Some old tramp. Thought that I was the Grim Reaper or something. Reckoned that I'd come to take him away.'

'What did you tell him?'

'Said that I'd come for someone else and that he'd better stay put tonight'.

'Good one.'

Lindsey shook her head. 'You two are weird.'

'Actually,' said Garrett. 'Talking about weird, can you go back to the old bum and give him a new command, you know, from the Angel of Death to his ears type of thing?'

Petrus grinned, 'Sure. What?'

Garrett told him.

Petrus ghosted back into the night.

A minute later Carlton heard a whisper of sound and he peeked out of his sleeping bag. The angel was there again, staring at him.

'Hey, no fair,' the old man said. 'You done say that you were gone and I just need to stay here and mind my own. You promised.'

'I have a task for you.'

'Oh. What?'

'Soon some men will come. You will know them when you see them. There will be many. Probably between ten and twenty. They will have modern weapons and will be wearing black. You will approach them. Do so openly and they will not harm you. You will tell them that they must go back. Tell them that this is not their fight. There is no need for them to die. Tell them that the Angel of Death has spoken. Do you understand?'

Carlton nodded. 'I understand.'

'Good. If they persist and they want to know where I am,' Petrus raised his spear and pointed. 'Tell them – I wait for them there.'

And once again Petrus disappeared into the dark.

Carlton sat and waited. Eager to do his task well, so as not to offend the death angel.

Petrus materialized out of the shadows and nodded to Garrett. 'Done,' he said. 'What exactly was that all about?'

'Three things,' said Garrett. 'Firstly, I hate killing mercenaries. They're just doing their job. Secondly, a bit of psychological warfare never hurt. Finally, it should bring them to us.'

Petrus sniffed. 'I don't mind killing mercs. They might only be doing their jobs but when their job is killing me, I take offence. You do realize that they'll know it's a trap? We've lost our element of surprise.'

'True, but we don't need it,' answered Garrett, in a disinterested fashion. 'I think that we should hide

Lindsey up here,' he continued indicating the thick copse of sweet chestnut trees that surrounded them. Devoid of much of their foliage but still surprisingly leafy.

Garrett laid out the tarpaulin and used his machete to slice it into two pieces. One length about three feet wide. Then he shinned up one of the largest trees, carrying the tarp and the rope with him, moving easily from branch to branch until he was about twenty feet up. Then he took the smaller piece of tarpaulin and tied it between two parallel branches, like a tight hammock or a canvas floor. He then looped the remaining canvas over the top in an A-frame. He tied the roof down and started to pull various branches around the tarpaulin and tie them down as well, creating a camouflage.

By the time he was finished, Lindsey couldn't see the hide at all.

Garrett called her up and she clambered up the broad boughed tree with ease.

'This is it,' he told her. 'You sit in here and wait for us.' He took a bottle of water and two chocolate bars out of his coat pocket. Then he stripped the wrapping off the bars so that, if Lindsey wanted any, there would be no sound of paper crumpling. After that, he pulled another small package from his pocket and opened it. 'Here, this is a space blanket. Well, actually it's the military version. Doesn't make noise like the civvie one. When I get down you wrap this around yourself. Right around, pull it over your head as well. It will ensure that they can't pick you up with their thermo goggles. Now don't come out until one of us tells you to. Okay?'

Lindsey nodded, her face grave.

'I'm serious,' stressed Garrett. 'I don't want one of those stupid movie situations where you don't listen and come to help us and fuck everything up, you hear me?'

'I won't move.'

'Hey,' called Petrus, 'If she says that she won't move then she won't.'

Garrett squeezed Lindsey's shoulder. 'Don't worry,' he reassured her. 'This is what we do. We'll sort this and after that we will find your dad.'

Then he climbed down, jumping the last ten feet.

Lindsey watched them vanish like some sort of magic trick. One moment they were there and then they were gone, no sound, no movement.

Simply gone.

As soon as they were undercover, Garrett grabbed Petrus by the shoulder. 'First thing,' he said as he opened the box of hand warmers. 'This is how they work.' Garrett grasped the top right-hand corner of the pack and pulled a tab. 'They heat up immediately and stay hot for about eight hours. After you activate them, you lay them out on the ground. Ten of them in a six-foot line. When a guy sees it through thermo-vision goggles, it looks like a person lying down and hiding. We've got enough to do about twenty fakes. Let's get to it. All around this area, it'll confuse them as well as lead them to us.'

Garrett held up a handful of six-inch steel nails and the roll of fishing line. 'Then of course, we've got these.'

'Wondered about those,' said Petrus. 'What are they for?'

'Simple spring trap,' answered Garrett. 'You cut down a sapling, inch or so diameter and three to four foot long. Knock a nail through the end so it sticks out at right angles. Then use another nail to attach the other end to a tree, parallel to the ground at thigh height. Tie a length of line to the end, pull it right back and then make a simple trip line so that when someone walks past, they trigger the sapling and, whack, six inches of sharpened steel in the thigh. Hurts like buggery and really difficult to pull out by yourself. In my experience most people that run into these tend to scream like a little girl and lose interest in pretty much anything else.'

Petrus grinned. 'I like it. Now, give me some of those warmers and you set those nail traps.'

The Zulu took a double handful of warmers and jogged off into the park, wrapping his bandana over his mouth before he went so as to ensure that no moisture clouds gave away his position.

CHAPTER TWENTY-SIX

There were twelve Watchmen left out of the original twenty-four. The Curator had called up all of them. However, one, a female Watchman of American origin, refused to take part. She claimed that the hit was way out of her area of expertise. Her refusal was totally acceptable and there would be no retribution. Watchmen were always at liberty to turn down a contract.

So now Daisy Van Staden sat in a VW Transporter with a driver and eleven Watchmen.

They carried either the Skorpion sub machine guns in a .32 caliber with a suppressor, or the HK MP5 silenced in 9mm.

Daisy had opted for a Russian Val silenced assault rifle. A relatively obscure weapon that he had gotten used to in the late 1990's. Accurate and silent and favored by the Russian Spetsnaz.

Three of the team had drawn the latest thermal vision night goggles that picked up body heat as well as light, giving a clear black and white image as opposed to the usual older green scifi image.

Daisy and the rest of the team had turned them down, they were bulky and awkward and tended to narrow one's vision. Sometimes in night ops it was better not to enhance one sense so far that it nullified the others. Night hunting was a game that needed sound and smell, as well as mere vision.

They all wore black cargo pants, black t-shirts and black three-quarter length wool jackets. No one wore body armor.

Happy had put Daisy in charge of the team. It was the first thing that he had said in the meeting and, if he had not, the huge Afrikaner would have probably turned the contract down. Because he alone knew what they were going up against.

And then Happy told them where the hit was to take place. Richmond Park. Over two thousand acres of bush. In the deep, frigid darkness of the English winter.

And Kobus 'Daisy' Van Staden had smiled to himself and shaken his head ruefully.

Happy snapped at him. 'We've got him, Van Staden,' he gloated. 'Caught on CCTV camera. Tried to disguise himself by wearing a baseball cap and shades, but we got him. It'll be a complete surprise, he's radically outnumbered. It will be a slaughter.'

And Daisy had nodded his agreement. The Curator was correct – it would be a slaughter.

But fighting was what Daisy did. It was all that he had ever known since he had been conscripted into the

South African defense force at sixteen years of age. He had never done anything else.

Ever.

And he was too old to start something new.

The VW pulled over in front of the gates to the park.

He took a deep breath and while everyone else climbed out he sat still for a while and said a silent prayer.

The same one that he and so many other soldiers had prayed since he had first entered the bloody fields of battle -

Do not forsake me, my Lord. For, even though I walk through the valley of the shadow of death, I will fear no evil, for you are with me and your rod and your staff will comfort me and protect me – amen.

Then he climbed from the car, keeping his weapon concealed under his open jacket and his fear concealed in his broken soul.

The Watchmen followed him into the park.

Into the darkness.

Into the shadow of death.

In the distance Kobus was sure that he heard a wolf like howl.

And he knew - His Lord had forsaken him.

With Daisy on point, the eleven Watchmen moved through the park, heading away from the gate and getting off the road as soon as they could. The place was empty. No one wanted to stroll around in the pitch-black freezing darkness of an English winter night. Well, no sane person, at any rate.

The big man stopped and beckoned all to him, dropping to one knee so that they had to huddle up. 'Right, guys,' he said. 'We've got two thousand acres of ground that the target could be hiding in. We've got to narrow that down. We'll start by checking out the best areas close to this gate. The targets have a similar background to most of us, so start by looking for the first place that you would choose. Right?'

There was a general mumble of agreement.

'Let's do it.'

As Daisy stood up and walked forward, a figure rose out of the bushes. The Afrikaner whipped his rifle up but as he did so it was obvious that this was not their target.

'Whoa,' he called out to his troops. 'Hold.'

Daisy looked closer and, by the feeble light of the moon he could see that the apparition was an old man, on his head a ragged watch cap, a sleeping bag wrapped around his shoulders. The whites of his eyes gleamed out in the darkness, two pools of ice-white in which floated two black pebbles.

'Step aside, old man,' said Daisy. 'Go back to sleep.'

'I have a message for you,' the old man said, his voice harsh. Scratchy. Like it was seldom used.

'No time, old man,' continued Daisy. 'Move.'

'You will have time for this,' said the old man. 'For it is a message from the Dark Angel himself. The angel who carries the spear of death.'

Daisy stopped in his tracks, as did the other Watchmen. All attention was turned to the tramp.

'Go on,' prompted Daisy.

'He has entrusted me to give you a message. He says, go home. To continue on your quest is death. He has no quarrel with you. This is not your fight and there is no shame in turning back. But if you continue, you will surely die.'

'Who said this to you?' blurted out Cornelius, another South African Watchman.

The old man stared at Cornelius. 'I already told you, man. The Angel of Death. He appeared to me. He let me live.'

'What did he look like?' asked Cornelius.

'He was tall. He was black. He carried a spear. He had no eyes and when he finished speaking, he disappeared into the night like that,' the old man snapped his fingers and Cornelius jumped. 'But before he left, he said, if you persisted then he would be waiting for you.' He pointed in the direction that Petrus had shown him. 'Over there.' Then the old man retreated back into the bush, going to ground like a cornered fox.

'Fuck this,' said Cornelius.

'What's the problem, Cornelius?' asked Daisy. 'Scared or something?'

Cornelius nodded. 'I don't like this. It's a trap. He'll be waiting for us.'

'So?'

'So, fuck this,' repeated Cornelius. 'These guys have taken out two of our kill teams without raising a sweat, and now they lure us here and tell us that they're waiting for us. Also, what's with this whole Angel of Death thing? I'm not happy.'

'Well then go,' said Daisy. 'If you're too scared, then leave,' continued the big man, hoping to shame Cornelius into action.

But Cornelius simply nodded and shouldered his weapon. 'Ja, you're right. I'm out of here.' He turned to the rest of the team. 'Trust me, guys. I've fought all over the world…these guys, they're something else. It doesn't matter how much we're being paid. You can't spend money when you're six feet under.' He walked back towards the gate, concealing his Skorpion under his coat as he did so.

There was an awkward silence and then Beatrice, the only other female Watchman, turned and followed him without a word.

Daisy shook his head. 'Anyone else?' he sneered in a voice that dripped with disgust.

The group of Watchmen shook their heads.

'Right then. Abraham,' Daisy said to one of the Israelis. 'You've got a pair of thermo goggles, put them on and check out that area that the old man showed us.'

Abraham had the bulky goggles hanging around his neck. It took him a couple of minutes to switch them on, don them and adjust the focus. He scanned the area and then gasped. A quick intake of air.

'What?' asked Daisy.

'There's a whole bunch of them,' answered Abraham. 'Ten, fifteen. Maybe more. Lying prone. They're hiding, but the goggles are picking them up fine.'

'That doesn't make sense,' said Daisy.

'Maybe it's someone else,' ventured Abraham.

'No ways,' denied Daisy. 'The old man said they're here. It must be them. They must have gotten reinforcements. Here, give me those goggles.'

Abraham handed them over and Daisy put them on, adjusting the focus to suit as he did so. He stared at the heat signatures for ages. They were faint but they were definitely there. He counted eighteen bodies, all prone, scattered seemingly arbitrarily around an area of maybe one acre or five thousand square yards.

The area was mostly covered in trees, mature woodland. On the periphery he suddenly saw movement and he concentrated on it. Another large group of heat signatures. Forty plus. Moving together into the designated area.

'What the hell is going on?' He whispered to himself. Then it came to him. Deer. A herd of deer. What about the other heat signatures? He wondered, did deer ever lie down? Could the prone figures be sleeping deer?

'Hey, guys,' he stage whispered. 'Who knows anything about deer?'

A man came forward; Daisy knew him but couldn't remember his name. Another South African, although an English speaker, not Afrikaans. Daniel, that was it.

'Ja, Daniel, tell me. Do deer sleep lying down?'

Daniel nodded. 'Ja, they sleep and they lie down. But they mainly sleep in the day, not at night. Well, they do in South Africa. Not that sure about here.'

'Take a look,' Daisy passed the goggles to Daniel.

After a few moments he gave them back. 'Could be deer. There could be two herds. One feeding, the other sleeping. There aren't any natural predators around here so their behavior will differ to the wild.'

'So, they could all be deer?'

'Ja.'

'Or people lying in wait?'

'Ja,' agreed Daniel. 'Except, the ones lying down, they're spread all over the place. If they were lying in ambush surely there would be some sort of pattern. You know, a V formation or something.'

'Unless it's a series of smaller ambushes,' mused Daisy. 'There's only one way to sort this out,' he continued. 'Form a line, twenty paces apart. We go soft and slow. When we get closer, go to ground, crawl forward. Let's get some face time with these thermal images. If it's a person and they're armed, take them out. Do it quick and keep going. Right, guys, time to earn our ridiculously high salaries.'

The Watchmen moved out.

They blended into the night, quiet and unobtrusive. Moving slowly, they all scanned the ground in front of them, checking for twigs or piles of leaves that may give away their position by creating noise. They had all done this many times before, and they were all still alive. That fact in itself meant they were all at the very pinnacle of their profession.

The best of the best.

And they outnumbered Garrett and Petrus almost five to one.

CHAPTER TWENTY-SEVEN

Daisy moved slowly and smoothly. Each step gliding over the grass, only inches high and then placing each foot down softly and carefully, ensuring that no twigs or leaves lay underfoot. Or something less innocuous, like a pungi stick - a sharpened stick placed in a small deep hole, or a booby trap or even a landmine.

His mind filled with the countless times that he had done this before, creeping through the bush in the dead of night. All senses on high alert. The sound of your own heartbeat thudding in your ears like Death's final countdown. Fear nibbling rat-like at your courage. Eating away at your being, slowly eroding your will to live.

Eroding your bravery.

They approached the treed area where Abraham had seen all of the prone figures and Daisy went to ground signaling for the others to do so as well. They crawled forward on hands and knees, still moving slowly. Their progress became glacial. Daisy cast his gaze about frantically, searching for one of the figures. But he saw nothing.

'This is impossible,' he said to himself. 'They were right here.'

He edged forward again and then stopped. Something felt wrong. Odd. He paused and let the night flow over him as he opened his senses.

And then it hit him…warmth. Close by. A human body? He stared at the area around him but still couldn't see anything. A superstitious thrill rippled through him. Now that he concentrated, he could definitely feel a living warmth right next to him.

He drew his blade from his belt, a Leatherneck SF, six and a half inches of cold steel death. Then he waved it over the heat. Nothing there. He plunged the blade into the turf. Nothing. But he could still feel the heat. Plucking up his courage he crawled directly over it. Then he saw it. A row of silver packets. He grabbed one. Hot.

Hand warmers.

'Shit,' he said to himself. 'It's a trap.'

At that same moment, about thirty yards away to Daisy's right, Abraham was coming to a similar conclusion. As he crawled forward, his thermo-vision goggles showed heat spots that could only be a person lying prone. But as he got closer, he lifted his goggles and peered around. There was nothing. He lowered the device and the image appeared again. He forced down the panic that was starting to rise within him.

There must be some sort of logical explanation.

So, with his heart hammering in his chest, he kept the goggles on and crawled forward.

He didn't notice the fishing line that he placed his hand onto as he crawled onwards. The taut line triggered the trap that Garrett had set earlier and the four-foot length of sapling whipped out and around, converting potential energy to kinetic energy.

By the time the six-inch steel nail struck Abraham, it was traveling at a speed of roughly two hundred and twenty feet per second. This imparted an energy of around one hundred feet pounds. In other words, it was traveling with enough energy to fell a small bear. The point of the nail pierced the right-hand lens of the thermo-goggles, shattered the glass and continued onwards, puncturing the eyeball, shattering the sphenoid bone and burying itself another four inches into the brain.

The pain was beyond anything that Abraham had ever come close to experiencing.

A high-pitched scream tore itself from his throat as he scrambled ineffectually at his face. But the nail was lodged firmly in him and the pressure of the sapling ensured that he couldn't pull it out.

And then the shadows around him coalesced into a human shape.

Daisy heard the blood curdling scream. Then it was cut off, fading to a strangled gurgle. The unmistakable sound of someone drowning in their own blood.

The next scream was further away. On the left at the very end of the line. This one ended more abruptly with the sound of steel striking flesh.

Then the sound of a Skorpion on full auto. A frantic clatter of sound. Four seconds. The sound of someone burning off an entire mag at once. Like a child using a rattle to scare away the monsters.

The men on each side of Daisy ran over, seeking support. An Israeli by the name of Maxim and an American ex Ranger named Stewart.

'What the fuck is going on?' asked Maxim.

'Stay cool,' commanded Daisy. 'There's only two of them. Look,' he held up a hand warmer. 'Heat packs. They used them to baffle our optics. Eyes skinned, boys. They're out there and they'll be moving. Get down.'

The three men lay prone, scanning the surrounds.

On the left another burst of automatic fire tore through the night followed by another gargled scream.

'You two,' said Daisy. 'Go left. I'll keep going forward and then flank left, maybe we can trap these buggers between us.'

Daisy moved forward, keeping a look out for booby traps as he did so.

Stewart and Maxim leopard crawled off to the left, keeping low and propelling themselves with their knees and elbows, weapons cradled in their arms and ready to fire.

Stewart took point with Maxim about five yards behind him. Neither man had the thermo imaging goggles, trusting to their natural senses instead.

As they moved forward, Stewart thought he heard a sound to his rear. A muted scuffle. He turned around to confer with Maxim.

But the Israeli was no longer there.

Stewart frantically scanned around for him, crawling back along their tracks. It was no good, his fellow mercenary had simply disappeared.

He heard another vague sound to his right and he snapped off a quick burst of fire in the general direction.

Another sound behind him. Fire, fire. Change magazines. Wait.

The whisper of steel. A blinding flash of red light exploded behind his eyes.

Blood. Pain.

Death.

Garrett checked Stewart's pulse.

Still.

He slid off into the night. A silent hunter. Death on gossamer steps.

A few hundred yards away another man died as he crawled through the long grass. A sliver of moonlight on sharpened iron. A muscled arm lunging forward out of the shadow. The shredded whisper of steel rending flesh. The gentle sigh of a soul escaping its earthly bonds.

Daisy could hear the sounds of his men dying all around him, but there was nothing he could do to stop it.

The Beast and his companion were running free, and it was far beyond a normal man's capacity to put a stop to them.

He lay low and waited, sweat trickling down his ice-cold face like a liquid distillation of his innermost fears.

And then he was there. Standing in front of him, his head cocked to one side. An old Sten gun grasped loosely in his right hand. A blooded machete tucked into his belt.

Van Staden stood up. Slowly.

Another man appeared next to Garrett. A black man. He held an assegai in his right hand. His face was blank. Devoid of expression.

Then the black man spoke.

'It is done,' he said. 'They are no more. There is only this one.'

Garrett continued to stare. Eventually he said. 'Daisy?'

A genuine question. Not a statement.

Daisy nodded. 'Yes, boss. It's me.'

'What are you doing here?'

'Hunting you, boss.'

Garrett smiled. Daisy was always the one to take every question as completely literal. 'Fair enough. What now?'

Daisy shrugged.

'Tell you what, Daisy,' said Garrett. 'Drop the weapon. Turn around and leave. There's no need to die.'

'I don't mind dying,' said Daisy, his face a mask of acceptance. 'It's the living that has become too hard to take.'

Tears started to run unbidden down the huge Afrikaner's face. The moonlight picked them up and turned them into blue sparkling tracks of liquid beauty.

Garrett shook his head. 'No, Daisy. Don't.'

Daisy shook his head, his eyes filled with emotion. A bitter sadness of a life that could have been. Of an existence lost to war and destruction. Friendless, without family. No future beyond the next kill. The next slaying.

And he moved. He was fast.

The only reason he had stayed alive so long was because he was preternaturally quick. The Russian Val whipped up and Daisy's finger tightened on the trigger.

But before he could squeeze off a shot the Sten barked. Three 9mm rounds struck the big man high up on his chest, punching him backwards and throwing him to the ground.

Garrett ran up and knelt next to him.

'Oh no, Daisy,' he whispered. 'Why?'

'I didn't know what else to do,' coughed the big man.

'You could have walked away.'

He shook his head and smiled. 'No, I couldn't. You know that better than anyone.'

Garrett smiled back. Nodded his understanding.

'Are you in pain?'

'No. I'm dying though.'

Garrett nodded. 'Yes, you are.'

'Boss, why did you leave us? Back in Sierra Leone. Why did you go? Our world went to shit after you left. The army fell apart, and we had to high tail it to the border. Lost half of the guys fighting our way out.'

'I know,' said Garrett. 'I'm sorry. I had to go. I could no longer handle what I had become.'

'*Popobawa*,' whispered Daisy. 'The Beast.'

Garrett nodded.

'You shouldn't have left us, boss.'

Garrett stroked Daisy's forehead. He said nothing. There was nothing to say. He had abandoned them. He knew that.

'Boss,' said Daisy, his voice a mere movement of air. Almost a sigh.

'Yes, I'm here.'

'I work for a company called The Custodian Group. International hit squad. The CEO is a guy called Nigel Taylor. Canada Square, Canary Wharf. I don't know why there's a hit out on you. I have no idea what this is all about. Mister Taylor will tell you.'

'Thank you, my friend,' said Garrett. 'Petrus and I will pay him a visit.'

'Another thing, Boss.'

'What?'

'A man who releases the beast in himself often does it so that he can get rid of the pain of being a man,' whispered Daisy. 'Be careful, my friend. Being a man is pain. To be human is pain. The pain means that we are alive.'

He squeezed Garrett's hand and smiled.

'Pretty philosophical for an old soldier, hey boss?' laughed the big man, weakly.

Garrett knelt next to Daisy for another five minutes.

Eventually Petrus spoke. 'He is dead.'

'I know,' breathed Garrett. 'I know.' He stood up and shouldered his Sten gun. 'We're going to have to do something about all of these bodies. As soon as they're found all hell will break loose. The cops will mobilize everyone, including the boy scouts and the girl guides.'

'What do we do?' asked Petrus.

'Come on, first we pick them up and put them there,' Garrett pointed to a natural depression in the ground. Then I have a plan.'

It took the two men just under half an hour to lay all of the dead mercenaries into the depression. After that, Garrett used his machete to cut down some tree branches that he laid over the bodies. Then he cut some lengths of rope and bent a few saplings over, tying them to form a natural looking copse.

Petrus was impressed. From a few yards away the bodies were completely hidden. And the depression was well off the usual tracks so he doubted that any casual passerby would see the mass grave.

Then Garrett took a small can out of his pocket. It was the blue aerosol can of Doggy-go-Away dog deterrent that he had purchased earlier. He sprayed the whole area around the bodies with a liberal dose of the chemical, keeping his finger on the nozzle until the can ran empty.

'There,' he said. 'That will stop any dogs paying attention. Should hopefully give us a few days, with any luck. Now, go and fetch Lindsey,' he continued. 'I'm going to cut the unused traps that I set. Can't have members of the public skewering themselves.'

'Okay,' said Petrus. 'We'll see you at the gate.'

Garrett walked off into the night and Petrus jogged to the foot of Lindsey's tree hide.

'Hey, Princess,' he called. 'It's done. Come on down.'

There was a noise and the young girl came shinning down the tree, landing lightly at Petrus' side.

'Are you alright?' she asked with concern.

'Yep.'

'And Garrett?'

'He's fine. No wounds. Let's go, he's meeting us at the gate.'

The two of them walked back towards the entrance. Lindsey walked in silence, almost like an automaton, seemingly oblivious of her surroundings. And then suddenly she started to shake violently, so much so that her teeth were starting to chatter together.

Petrus put his arm around her. 'Are you alright, Princess?'

She nodded. 'Cold. That's all.'

The Zulu knew that she was starting to react to shock and he cursed himself for not being gentler with her. Her wit and upbeat demeanor meant he was guilty of treating her more like an adult than a little girl.

He knelt next to her and put his arms around her, holding her tight until the shivers died down.

'Thanks,' she whispered. 'Better now.'

Petrus stood up and they continued on their way.

When they were close to the gate Petrus motioned for Lindsey to stop.

'I'm just going to have a quick chat to someone,' he said. 'You wait here. Don't be nervous, you're safe. There's no one left to cause a problem. Trust me.' He grinned.

Lindsey stood still and Petrus went over to the old tramp's hideaway.

'Hey, old man,' he called.

No one answered.

'Hey,' repeated Petrus. 'Just wanted to tell you that it's over. If you want to move around you can.'

The Zulu pushed his way into the bush. He could see the old man lying on the ground. Still.

Petrus nudged him, pushing his shoulder with his right hand.

The old man stayed still.

Petrus moved forward and knelt over him, rolling him onto his back as he did so.

In the very center of the old man's forehead was a ragged hole. A stray round from the fire fight had hit him right between the eyes. Killing him instantly.

Petrus took in a deep breath, holding it for a while as he tried to control the rage that washed over him like a tsunami.

He had told the old man not to move. He had told him that he would be safe.

He had lied.

The Zulu stood up.

Someone was going to pay for this.

He went back to Lindsey and walked her to the entrance.

Try as he might, Happy was unable to contact anyone from the kill team that he sent to Richmond Park. Every mobile phone either went straight through to messages or simply rang until it switched off. Even Daisy's emergency phone that was always kept on.

He had been able to contact Cornelius who had broken off the contact just before he had gone in. But he had been no help, giving Happy a garbled story about an old black man, an angel of death and a trap of some sorts. Then he simply cut Happy off and refused to answer again.

It looked like the absolute impossible had actually happed. And Taylor had to admit it – the targets had taken out his kill team. In the matter of a few days, his entire stock of Watchmen, hard international assassins, had been retired.

Sweat ran down the Curator's face and trickled onto the collar of his shirt. It was the rancid sweat of fear. And defeat. But mainly fear, because Happy Taylor knew he now had no one to protect him and, although he was no mean warrior himself, he was pragmatic enough to know that these men were his martial superiors in every way.

So, with ear fumbling fingers, he took out his phone and punched in a series of numbers. It was time to call in the ultimate help.

Time to pay the piper.

Happy had used the man only once before and, truth be told, he scared the living shit out of the old veteran.

His name was Bastien Zumthor, and he worked with a younger assistant, Yohan Wyss.

Zumthor was Swedish, blonde, six foot two, well built.

Wyss a youthful replica of his master. They were not part of a company and they worked for whoever paid them. Their minimum fee was half a million dollars, paid on completion of the task. They always completed their tasks.

Zumthor answered and Taylor told him of his dilemma, leaving out none of the details.

'I shall get back to you with half an hour,' replied the assassin in his sing song Swedish accent.

Happy disconnected and then sat back, staring at the phone like it was his only lifeline in a sea of shit. He willed it to ring. Trying to get time to pass more quickly.

When the phone rang, he answered immediately.

'Yes, talk to me.'

'My dear mister Taylor. You are indeed in deep trouble, my friend. I had to call in a few favors but I now know exactly who we are dealing with. The two men are named Garrett, and Petrus. To put it mildly – they are very bad news. I am definitely going to need my assistant in on this one. I will leave now for London on my own jet, ETA within two hours. The cost for this is seven hundred and fifty thousand dollars, payable on completion as always. Is that acceptable?'

Happy did some quick mental accounting before answering. 'Yes, Bastien, that will be fine.'

'Good. I will see you soon. One last thing. Mister Taylor, I have told you before – you do not get to use my first name. We are not friends.'

'Of course, I am sorry, mister Zumthor.'

'Fine, it is not a disaster; we must all remember our places, should we not? After all, we would all prefer to avoid anarchy.'

Zumthor chuckled and disconnected the call.

Happy stared at the phone for a few seconds and then threw it against the wall. 'Arrogant asshole,' he shouted at the inanimate object.

Happy opened his top drawer and took out 9mm Glock. He checked the load and then slipped it into his belt.

Then he selected a cigar from the large ornate humidor that sat on his desk top, cut the end off and lit it.

Standing up he paced the room for a while, clearing his mind and attempting to calm his racing heart.

After half an hour of pointless pacing he sat down at his desk, but that was even worse so, once again he stood up and paced the room, lighting another cigar as soon as the first was finished.

Almost exactly two hours had passed when the security intercom buzzed. Happy pushed the button.

'Yes.'

'It is Zumthor and Wyss.'

'Come in,' said Happy as he pushed the button that unlocked the door.

The two Swedes walked in. They radiated both confidence and arrogance in equal measure. Assured in the fact that they were the very best of the best in their chosen profession.

Wyss stood forward and placed a briefcase on the desk while Zumthor cast his gaze about, taking in the office and its furnishings.

Deep pile, cream Wilton wool carpets, English Oak wood paneled walls, recessed lights. A fake gas fireplace. Above it an original Picasso pencil drawing in a heavy frame. The furniture a mix of genuine antiques and very good reproductions.

The Swede smirked at the effort, comparing it to his Spartan office at home with its clean lines, seaweed mating and original Klimt. As opposed to this clumsy middle class attempt at sumptuousness.

'So,' he said to Taylor. 'Still persisting in your attempt to turn death into a corporate entity, I see.'

Happy shrugged.

'You dress up an honorable calling in the robes of the merchant,' sneered Zumthor. 'Do you honestly think that by having a website, Google Adwords, and a corporate logo, you will give what we do a veneer of societal acceptance? It is a farce. What we do will never be understood by the masses because we are so far above them. By making an attempt at inclusivity you merely denigrate a noble profession. From 1090 when the first Order of Assassins was formed, through to the Black Hand society, the Knights of the Golden Circle and the Illuminati.'

Zumthor walked over to the window and looked out at the Thames and the city beyond, lit up in an orgy of neon.

'I speak six languages and I play three musical instruments. I ride, fly and ski. Killing is an art, not the almost animalistic sexual act that you people have turned it into.'

'It is what it is,' retorted Taylor. 'It pays the bills.'

'Crass commercialism,' snapped Zumthor. 'Now these two men that we wait for. True artists. Not subtle, that is true. More Dadaism than Turner, but still true proponents of the art.'

The assassin walked over to Happy's desk and, without being offered, opened the humidor and selected a Romeo y Juliet half corona. He flicked his wrist and a small blade appeared in his hand. With a single deft movement, he trimmed the end of the cigar off and flicked the tip into the ashtray. The blade magically disappeared to be replaced with a golden Dunhill lighter. He took his time lighting and then walked back to the window to survey the view once more.

'Garrett is a soldier of fortune. He has operated throughout most of Africa as well as a short stint in Europe. In the Dark Continent he is often referred to as "The Beast", a nickname earned through his use of almost unbelievable violence to achieve his goals. He is a true killing machine, but a man with honor, with a sense of justice. No matter that it is warped, it is still there. A true champion of the people.'

Happy could see that Zumthor was getting visibly excited as he talked about his adversary. His color was high and his breath had quickened slightly. Like a sailor looking at a naked woman after a month at sea. It made the Curator feel slightly nauseous. Ill at ease.

'Yes,' continued Zumthor. 'This will definitely be my ultimate kill. The trophy of all trophies.'

He licked his lips and then took a huge drag on the cigar, rolling the smoke around in his mouth before letting it trickle out like a vapid waterfall.

'The Zulu is different,' he said. 'More primal. Less complex. Easier to anger and quicker to kill. He is a man who will kill without compunction or remorse. Because of that he is less dangerous than the enigmatic Beast. You see, the very uncontrollability of The Beast is what gives Garrett his power. His…authority. Yes, I will gift the Zulu to Yohan. It will be well within his capabilities and, at the same time provide him with a worthy notch on his gun.'

As Zumthor finished his soliloquy the door to the office literally exploded in, the hinges shattering under a fusillade of bullets as Garrett and Petrus pumped a full magazine each into them, tearing the metal from the door.

Happy jumped behind his desk, but neither Zumthor nor Wyss flinched. They both simply turned to face the door.

Zumthor took a puff of his cigar before laying it in the ashtray. 'Welcome, gentlemen,' he said. 'My name is Bastien Zumthor and this is my colleague and assistant, Yohan Wyss. Please call me Bastien. I in turn, will call you Garrett and Petrus, I hope that does not offend.' The assassin turned to his assistant. 'Yohan, please step forward.'

The younger Swede took two steps forward and bowed slightly.

'Petrus,' continued Zumthor. 'I hope that you don't mind, but I have placed you against Yohan. I believe it will be a good, but fair match.'

Petrus looked at Garrett. 'Do you have any idea what this dickhead is talking about?'

Garrett shrugged, and shook his head without replying.

Yohan shook his arms and rolled his head to work any kinks out of his neck and then, without warning, he drew two large butterfly knives, the bright steel spinning and glittering in his hands as he spun the blades, moving forward at the same time.

Petrus dropped his empty Sten gun and whipped out his assegai, holding it in his right hand, standing on the balls of his feet as the Swedish assassin wove a deadly dance of steel and light in front of him.

Yohan moved slowly to his right, looking to flank the Zulu, his knives still whirling and flashing in a huge display of skill, forming an impenetrable curtain of spinning razor-sharp steel.

Petrus tracked right with him and then he simply ran straight at Yohan. The assistant whipped a blade up and forward but Petrus threw his forearm at the trajectory of the blade and allowed it to penetrate deep into his flesh. Then he tensed his arm muscles to lock the blade in place.

At the same time, he stepped forward and slammed his assegai into Yohan's chest, twisted it savagely and then withdrew the blade in a fountain of blood.

Yohan didn't even have time to look surprised before his dead body fell to the floor.

Petrus pulled the butterfly knife out of his forearm with a grunt and threw it onto Yohan's prostrate corpse.

'You bring toys to a fight,' the Zulu sneered. 'You stupid child. Truly, you have no fucking idea, do you?'

'Impressive,' admitted Bastien, his cold blue eyes betraying no emotion whatsoever. 'Yes, very primal. However,' he continued. 'I think that you will find that I am not Yohan.'

Garrett shook his head at Petrus. 'Really?' He asked. 'That was the best idea that you could come up with?'

Petrus tore off a strip from his shirt sleeve and tied it tightly around the wound. 'Rush of blood to the head,' he said embarrassedly. 'Made me go all macho.'

Bastien walked over to the desk, opened the brief case and took out what looked to be a short sword. He swung it a few times to loosen up his shoulder muscles.

'Garrett,' he said. 'This is a copy of a Roman Gladius. My research led me to believe that you are considered some sort of aficionada of the Machete. A savage instrument, but effective. I shall put my Gladius up against it. I feel that it is the most appropriate blade from my collection. Roman might, up against African savagery.'

The master assassin held the blade up in front of his face in a salute and then swished it down. 'Sir, let the best man win.'

Garrett pulled the Walther P99 from his belt and double tapped Bastien in the chest.

The assassin dropped his blade and fell to his knees, a look of complete and utter surprise on his face.

'You shot me,' he gasped.

'Of course I did,' agreed Garrett.

'Why?'

'Had to, before you bored me to death.'

'But there is no honor in this.'

'You're right,' agreed Garrett. 'But then, there never is.'

He pulled the trigger again, a single shot between Zumthor's eyes.

Dead.

Then Garrett swiveled and shot Happy in his right thigh. Happy fell to the floor with a grunt of pain.

'Hey, what the fuck?' he exclaimed. 'There was no need to shoot me.'

'Maybe, maybe not,' said Garrett. 'Tell me, who were these clowns? Bloody Laurel and Hardy double act.'

'Assassins,' answered Happy. 'Best in Europe. Bastien Zumthor and Yohan Wyss, the go-to-guys when the shit hits the fan.'

'Useless pair of jokers if you ask me,' said Garrett.

Happy nodded. 'I am forced to agree with you. They have been a great disappointment to me.'

'I take it that you are Happy Taylor.'

'That's me. Look, could I get a bandage. I really am bleeding rather badly here.'

Garrett shook his head. 'No. Take your belt off, make a tourniquet. We won't be long.'

Happy stripped his belt off and tied it around his thigh, grimacing at the pain as he did so.

'Okay,' said Garrett. 'Information time. Why and who and what?'

Happy shook his head. 'I can give you the who and the what, but I have no idea about the why, genuinely.'

'Start with what you know then,' commanded Garrett

'It's a woman, name of Debra Haddock. Big noise politician. Real cow. She's the only contact that I've had on this one.'

'Where does she live?'

Happy shook his head. 'No idea. But she's a big noise. Shouldn't be hard to find her. Now the what – simple, we were hired to off you, and the Zulu, and a little girl. That's all.'

'Okay,' said Garrett. 'Now – why?'

'Don't know.'

'Of course you do.'

'I swear. Jesus, man. Why would I withhold info? I'm a fucking hired gun, there's no sense of allegiance here, I swear.'

'Speculate.'

'She's a big hitter and they aren't sparing any expense. I reckon you've pissed off someone really high up. Man, what did you do, kill a politician?'

Garrett shook his head. 'Doesn't matter. Where do you stand on this?'

'In what way?'

'Are you going to continue trying to kill us?'

Happy shook his head. 'No way. I'm rescinding the contract as of immediately.'

Garrett nodded. 'Good idea.'

'Anyway,' continued the Curator ruefully. 'You guys have killed twenty-five of my people so the point is moot. I basically don't have a work force anymore.'

'Right then,' said Garrett. 'We're out of here. I trust that no one will follow us.'

Happy nodded.

Garrett turned and Petrus led the way out.

As they got to the door Garrett stopped, his head cocked to one side. He slowly turned and looked at Happy again. 'Twenty-five?' He asked.

'Yep,' agreed Happy as he tightened his tourniquet.

'But even if I count these two clowns here, we've only done nineteen,' observed Garrett.

Happy nodded his agreement. 'True. The other six were killed in a house in the Elephant and Castle. We sent a team to get you and they ran into some giant who offed the whole team.'

'What happened to the giant? asked Garrett, his voice dull. Emotionless.

'He died,' said Happy in an offhand way. 'Got gut shot during the firefight.'

Garrett pulled the Walther from his belt again and fired in one smooth motion. The bullet struck the Curator in the left elbow, shattering it completely. He screamed in agony.

'He was my friend,' said Garrett as he fired again.

Happy's right elbow disintegrated in a pink spray of blood and bone chips.

He fell to the carpeted floor and writhed about, keening in pain.

Garrett stood over him. 'Look at me' he commanded, his voice more animal growl than human diction.

The Curator dragged his pain filled eyes up to Garrett's face.

And he stared upon the countenance of The Beast.

'You killed my friend,' growled The Beast.

And he shot the Curator in the face, pulling the trigger repeatedly until the slide wracked back and the magazine was empty.

CHAPTER TWENTY-NINE

Lindsey found Debra Haddock's website, complete with her official schedule and contact address. Unfortunately, the contact address was not her home address, but they did know when she would be in parliament or at certain speeches.

So, they simply waited for her outside of an official engagement in the East of London. The opening of a new youth center, a club planned to lift and enrich the lives of inner-city kids. But in reality, just another building that would become a gang-controlled crack joint. Or simply a rundown concrete hulk covered in graffiti and piss.

They waited for Haddock, her driver and her bodyguard to get into the car and then Garrett prepared to pull out after them, but Petrus stopped him.

'Check it out,' he said. 'There's a second car with two more bodyguards. Wait for them before you pull off.'

'This is unusual,' said Garrett. 'So many bodyguards for a mere backbencher. Must be private. Ex-special forces, or current would be my guess.'

'What' s so unusual about that?' asked Petrus. 'In South Africa all the ministers have a bigger entourage than Kanye West.'

'Yeah, well this isn't Africa, and Kanye West is an asshole.'

Lindsey and Garrett high fived and laughed.

Then Garrett pulled out to follow Haddock.

The convoy of cars meandered through London, heading east, past Greenwich and on, into a light industrial area.

The winter sun was already going down and Garrett switched on his lights to dispel the encroaching darkness.

As they drove, Garrett held well back, almost losing Haddock at times in his attempt to remain unseen.

Eventually the two cars pulled into an industrial complex. It was well run down, many vacant warehouses, little lighting and a general air of disuse.

Haddock's car parked next to one of the warehouses and her bodyguards in the second car pulled up behind her.

There were four more cars in the parking area.

Garrett pulled over, a fair distance away, and he watched as Haddock's bodyguards got out of the cars and scanned the area.

There was no way they could easily see him as his lights were off and he was parked behind a series of chain link fences.

The entourage trooped inside, closing the front door behind them.

'Should we scout the place,' asked Petrus.

'No,' said Garrett. 'Let's sit tight and wait a bit. Those other cars bother me. Bound to be more fire power inside the building, plus Haddock's heavies. Not that keen to risk another firefight without good reason.'

Petrus nodded his agreement. 'Right then' he said. 'Let's wait.'

Debra strode into the building, flanked by sergeant Robhurst and trailed by her two other bodyguards and her driver.

She walked towards the workshop and Robhurst stepped forward and opened the door for her.

The colonel and the commander sat on a pair of office chairs, over in a corner, chatting to themselves. Professor Parker stood next to a workbench. In front of him, a small circuit board in a bench vice, in his hand a soldering iron.

Both the commander and the colonel looked up, surprised at Haddock's aggressive entrance.

Debra pointed at the professor. 'Hit him,' she commanded.

Robhurst walked over and, without a change of expression spun the professor around and punched him in the stomach. The prof dropped the soldering iron and fell to the floor, struggling to breath.

'Why is the devise not ready yet?' asked Debra.

Bradley Parker shook his head. 'I'm working as fast as I can, you rancorous old sow,' he spluttered. 'It's close.'

Debra turned to Robhurst. 'Sergeant, take my car, go to the professor's daughter and cut off both of her thumbs. Bring them straight back here.'

After a slight flicker of hesitation, Robhurst nodded.

Parker rose to his knees. 'No,' he shouted, his voice shrill with desperation. 'Please, no. It'll be ready tomorrow, I swear it. Please.'

Debra stared at him for a while and then nodded. 'Tomorrow, or that's it. End of the lollipop, professor. After that, I swear, we will cut Lindsey's limbs off.'

Parker shook his head, tears glistening in his eyes. 'No – tomorrow, I promise.'

Debra beckoned to the commander and the colonel, gesturing towards the door with a tilt of her head.

She walked from the room and they followed her. Omegas to her Alpha. Robhurst prowled behind them.

'Tomorrow is D-Day,' she instructed. 'And not a moment too soon, I tell you.'

'Why?' enquired commander Hastings.

'I'm getting a distinctly iffy feeling about this whole thing,' replied Debra. 'I've tried to contact The Custodian Group but the mobile number that I had no longer exists. I asked around and that has never happened before, not on any operation that the government have ever sanctioned.'

'Could just be a technical fault,' suggested the commander.

'Could be,' admitted Debra. 'But I prefer to expect the worst. If the targets have, by any chance, neutralized the Custodians then they will be after us next. I still have no idea who these people are or who they are working for. I suspect that something must have leaked, but to who? If it were our boys, MI5 or the CIA, then we would know. They'd be all over us, like ugly on a moose.'

'The Israelis?' suggested the commander

Colonel Peterson shook his head. 'Makes no sense. They would report to MI5, or simply take us out.'

'Look, gentlemen,' urged Haddock. 'It doesn't actually matter. The event horizon approaches and there is no turning back. No stopping us. Take all precautions, increase your personal security. We shall meet back here tomorrow at noon.'

Haddock left the building followed closely by Robhurst, her other bodyguards, the colonel, the commander and their respective protectors.

A conga line of well-armed, middle class, moral turpitude.

CHAPTER THIRTY-ONE

Garrett and Petrus watched the procession leave the warehouse.

Lindsey sat in the Land Rover while the two men crouched behind it, peering around the tires to gain sight of Debra and her accomplices.

Then Lindsey climbed carefully out of the Land Rover and took out her smart phone. She pointed it at the group and took a series of photographs, ensuring that the flash wasn't on so that it didn't give away their position.

'What's that for? asked Petrus. 'Holiday snaps?'

'Don't be so facetious,' snapped Lindsey. 'I can put their photos through Google images and maybe get a match of some sort. Find out who the other guys are.'

'Really, does that work?'

Lindsey shrugged. 'To be honest, I don't know. Just thought that it was worth a shot.'

Petrus turned to Garrett. 'So, which ones are we going to follow?'

Garrett shook his head. 'Neither. I want to see what's in the warehouse. We can pick up Haddock afterwards.'

They waited for the various members of Haddock's group to drive off, Debra with her following car of bodyguards, and the two other men, each with two bodyguards and a driver. A formidable force.

'Let's go,' said Garrett. 'Lindsey, wait in the car. We won't be long.'

'I hate waiting, that's all that I do is sit in cars hoping that you guys come back. I get scared.'

'Don't be scared, Princess,' said Petrus. 'We'll be as quick as we can. A fast search and back. See what we can pick up; maybe get to the bottom of this pile of shit. If you see anyone coming you honk the horn and we'll come running.'

'Okay,' mumbled Lindsey.

The two men faded into the night, heading towards the side of the warehouse, an area that was shrouded in shadow.

They crouched down below one of the cracked and filthy windows and then Garrett popped his head up and stole a quick glance inside.

'What do you see?' asked Petrus.

'Empty room. Open door. Lights in the corridor beyond. Saw some guy walking past. Shoulder holster, pistol. Nothing heavy'

'There could be another hundred in there,' said Petrus. 'They might have a bloody bus that drops them off every morning for all that we know.'

'Could be,' admitted Garrett. 'Could be that he's the only one. There is only one car outside.'

'True,' said Petrus. 'But there could be more cars around the back. In fact, if they're here on a semi-permanent basis then that's probably where the other cars would be. Only one way to find out for sure. Reckon that this is a good ingress point?'

'As good as any.'

'Let's do it.'

They drew their blades and Garrett checked for any alarm wires before he used his machete to lever up the sash window, slipping the catch and moving the window up in small silent increments.

Both men slipped into the room and walked over to the door, peering out into the lit corridor. It was empty and Garrett held his breath as he listened out for any sign of life. Voices, walking, anything.

Then he pointed. 'Down there,' he whispered. 'Voices. Behind that door at the end of the corridor.'

'Blades or bullets?' asked Petrus.

'Let's go in cold and quiet,' answered Garrett. 'If things start to deteriorate then we'll go weapons hot, but we'll try to keep it silent for now.'

'If we go in with blades then it's all or nothing,' said Petrus.

'What do you mean?'

'We'll have to kill them. Guys tend not to take you seriously when you point a spear at them and tell them to put their hands up.'

'True,' admitted Garrett. 'But the probability is that these guys are SAS or at least the pick of the bunch, so whatever we point at them they aren't going to go quietly.'

Petrus nodded. 'Let's do it.'

Garrett led the way down the corridor. They paused outside the door and listened for a few seconds. They could hear talking but it was impossible to tell how many men there were in the room.

Hoping for the best, Garrett placed his hand on the door handle, turned fast and smooth, pushed the door open and strode into the room, moving towards the right-hand side.

Petrus was close behind him, going left.

There were four men, and they reacted faster than Garrett would have believed possible.

Pistols were drawn and pointed within less than a second. But in that tiny slice of time that it took to draw and aim, Garrett had swung and connected. The machete slicing through the closest man's throat, opening his jugular and spraying the room with blood.

Petrus had moved even faster, slicing and stabbing in one continuous flow of movement. Both of the men on his side of the room fell to the floor. One had been eviscerated and the other stabbed through the heart. With a balletic spin he returned to the first man who lay thrashing on the floor in an attempt to push his entrails back into his stomach cavity. With a savage thrust he plunged his assegai into the juncture of the man's neck, smashing the clavicle bone and severing the carotid artery in a coup de gras.

There was a loud bang and Garrett staggered back, clutching his side. Petrus leapt onto the table and swung his assegai down like an axe, chopping into the last soldier's upper arm, almost severing it completely. Then, with an upward stroke, he rammed the wide blade into the man's throat, twisting it as he did so, killing him instantly.

Springing down from the table he ran to Garrett.

'Are you okay?'

Garrett nodded. 'Just a graze,' he said, clutching his left-hand side. Blood welled past his fingers and dripped to the floor. 'I hesitated, don't know why. Son of a bitch got me.'

'You're thinking too much,' said Petrus. 'Look, these men are our enemies; they would kill us without thought. You keep thinking and you'll get us both killed.'

Garrett nodded. 'Good point. Sorry.'

'Right,' urged Petrus. 'We had better move. Whoever else is in the building knows that we're here.'

Both of the men holstered their blades and unslung their silenced Sten guns.

'We can look at that wound when the job's done,' said Petrus. 'Until then, try to stop losing so much blood, you might slip on it and hurt yourself.'

'Ha ha,' responded Garrett. 'Very funny.'

The Zulu led the way into the corridor and they headed towards the front of the warehouse, keeping close to the walls, holding their sub machine guns ready, walking with deliberate steps.

On the right a door burst open and a man stepped out, firing as he did, Military issue Walther.

Both Petrus and Garrett opened up at the same time. Two quick bursts. The man was flung back into the room like he had a giant rubber band attached to him, dead before he hit the ground.

Just before the front entrance, the corridor doglegged to the right and the two men kept walking, slow and steady.

The door at the end of the corridor banged open and another man rolled through, rising up onto one knee before firing. But he was too slow and the Sten guns cut him down in a fusillade of fire.

Both Garrett and Petrus reloaded, dropping their spent magazines and slotting full ones back in.

Garrett looked at his friend. 'On three?'

'On three,' he agreed.

Garrett counted down and on three they leapt into the room, hitting the floor and rolling both left and right, scanning the room as they did so.

Garrett's Sten growled, and a man fell.

There was one more man in the room. He wore a stained white lab coat; his hair was disheveled.

He had both of his hands held high, like a child playing prisoner in a game of cowboys and Indians.

Garrett covered him whilst Petrus went to the door and checked for any more guards.

'Who are you?' asked Garrett.

'Parker,' answered the man. 'Bradley Parker. Please don't shoot me.'

Garrett smiled. 'Lindsey's dad?'

The professor looked baffled. 'You know my daughter?'

'Sure do,' said Petrus. 'She's the reason that we're here.'

'I don't understand. How? Why?'

Petrus chuckled. 'Put your hands down, prof. Your daughter is safe. In fact, she's outside, waiting for us.'

The professor still looked baffled. 'She can't be.'

'She is,' corrected Petrus. 'Come on, looks like it's a good time to split this place. I reckon that we've taken care of all of the opposition.'

Bradley followed the two friends out of the building and into the car park. Then across the area of crumbling blacktop and onto the adjacent road.

They were still ten yards from the Land Rover when the door opened and Lindsey came running towards them.

'Daddy,' she squealed. 'Is that you?'

Bradley shambled into an exhausted run to cover the last few feet, picking up his daughter and holding her tight.

Lindsey was laughing and crying at the same time. Bradley simply held her, also laughing although tears streamed down his face as he did so.

Eventually he put her down and grabbed her right hand, then her left.

'But, your fingers,' he said. 'They're all there.'

Lindsey did a double take at the complete non sequitur.

'Umm, yes, daddy,' she said. 'Why wouldn't they be?'

Bradley stared at his daughter's hands for a while longer, then slowly sat down, his legs simply giving way in the face of his massive confusion. Legs splayed out in front of him like a child in a sandpit.

'I'm perplexed,' he said, shaking his head. 'Whose finger? When did...' He rubbed his eyes with the heels of his hands. 'Who are these men?'

'They're good friends, daddy. But that can all be explained later. I think that we should get out of here.'

'I agree,' confirmed Garrett. 'We have no idea when more uglies might pitch up.'

Bradley shook his head. 'No, wait. We can't go.'

'Why?' asked Garrett.

'The workshop. There's stuff that I need.'

'Look, prof,' said Garrett. 'Whatever you need we can buy. It's more important to get out of here.'

Bradley shook his head again. 'You don't understand.' He pointed at the warehouse. 'In there...it's a nuclear bomb and it's almost complete.'

Garrett went pale. 'A nuclear bomb?'

'Yes. Small, portable, deadly. And almost good to go. We've got to go back and make sure that it can't be used.'

Garrett nodded. 'Let's go. Petrus, stay with Princess,' he said as he led the way back into the building.

Bradley went straight to the workshop and walked up to a large metal frame from which a spherical steel ball hung. When Garrett got closer, he could see that the ball was actually a series of octagonal plates joined together. Out of each plate ran two wires that led to a junction box and a bird's nest of multicolored wires.

Professor Parker began pulling wires out, seemingly at random.

'Hey, careful,' warned Garrett. 'I hope that you know what you're doing.'

The prof paused momentarily to send a scathing look his way.

'Sorry,' apologized Garrett sheepishly.

After a few minutes Bradley rushed over to another work bench and picked up a small container. He went back to the bomb and started to disassemble parts of it, then, after donning a pair of heavy gloves, he extricated a small ball slightly larger than a tennis ball and he placed it into the container. After that he picked up another small metal phial and popped that in as well.

Then he laid the various parts that he had disconnected out along the workbench top and he started to connect new wires to them.

'Uh, prof,' said Garrett. 'I don't want to upset you but I feel that we are a little pushed for time here.'

'Another minute,' snapped the professor. 'We simply cannot leave anything here for these people to use.'

He connected the last two wires and then ran them to a box that had a flashing red light and a small antenna on it. Finally, he picked up the container and a small black object that looked to Garrett like a garage door remote, placing both into the pockets of his lab coat.

'Right, all done,' murmured the professor as he picked up the container. 'Let's go.'

Garrett led the way out of the building, checking for any resistance as he went. They made it safely back to the car without incident.

'Great,' said Petrus. 'Can we go now?'

'Yes, we can,' confirmed Bradley. 'Just one more thing.' He turned to face the building, raised the small black remote and pushed a button.

A series of thumping explosions rippled through the building and then the entire structure simply folded in on itself.

'What the fuck,' shouted Garrett. 'What did you do?'

'Had to destroy any chance of them reconstructing what I had done,' said the professor.

'Yeah, well you could have warned us,' said Garrett.

They all clambered into the Land Rover and Garrett pulled off.

In the back seat Lindsey leaned against her father for a while, then she sat up straight and opened the window.

'Daddy,' she said. 'Don't take this the wrong way, but you really need a bath.'

Bradley laughed. 'Trust me, my darling,' he said. 'I know that better than anyone else, after all, my body odor is directly under my own nose.'

'You can have a shower when we get to a hotel,' said Garrett. 'It won't be long now.'

'Well, I appreciate that,' said Bradley. 'But I rather think that we should and see someone. Some government body that we can report this all to.'

'Sorry, buddy,' said Garrett. 'No can do.'

'Why?'

'Because it's not only the cops in on this whole thing. As you know, it's the army and some politicians, the media and who knows what other organization. At the moment I wouldn't stake my life, and yours, on anyone. Not MI5, MI6…no one. Seriously, prof, I cannot tell you how many men have being trying to kick our butts over the last few days. Look, I'll find a hotel that suits us, you shower, I'll order some food and then we can all sit down and discuss what's going on. Both sides of the story, yours and ours. Happy?'

Bradley nodded. 'Sounds like the correct thing to do. Thank you very much.'

'Not a problem,' responded Garrett.

Garrett headed to the outskirts of London, off the beaten track a little and finally pulled over into a budget hotel next to a highway service station.

'This place looks pretty discreet,' he said. 'I'll go and book two rooms, you lot wait here.'

After Bradley showered, Garrett gave him a set of his clothes. They were of a similar height, but Garrett's arms and shoulders were almost twice the size of the skinny scientist and the clothes hung on him like the skin on a Shar-Pei puppy. But at least they were clean.

Then Petrus took care of Garrett's wound, cleaning it roughly, and then stitching it up using the hotels free sewing kit. Lindsey watched in fascination as the Zulu put six deft stitches into Garrett, his big hands working with care and precision.

'Wow,' she exclaimed. 'You're really good at that.'

Petrus grinned. 'Lots of practice,' he answered as he laid a bandage over the wound.

After that, it took almost two hours to tell Bradley the whole story and get him completely up to date.

Then he recounted his end of the tale up until their rescue.

'So whose finger did they show you?' asked Petrus.

'Must have been some random child,' said Garrett, his eye glittering with subdued anger. 'Must have killed her afterwards or we would have heard something about it in the news.'

'It would have been sergeant Robhurst,' said Bradley. 'SAS soldier, Haddock's bodyguard, complete psycho. Beat the crap out of me a couple of times.'

'He's a dead man,' snarled Garrett. 'He just doesn't know it yet.'

'Guys,' interjected Lindsey. 'I think that you're missing the point here. We're talking about a group of people that were planning to explode a fucking nuclear weapon on British soil.'

'Language,' barked Garrett and Petrus together.

Bradley grinned at the reaction from the two men.

'I can assure you, Lindsey,' said Garrett. 'That point has not evaded us. And I can assure you that this group of people will not go unpunished. But before we all go off halfcocked we need to be fully prepared. Bradley, do you know the names and addresses of the major players involved?'

Bradley shook his head. 'I know names, a bit of info, but that's all.'

'Okay, shoot.'

'The woman, you already know. Councilor Debra Haddock. Then there are two men. Police Commander, City of London police. Name of Jarvis Hastings. Then there's a Colonel Grant Peterson, 21 SAS. Look, gentlemen,' continued Bradley. 'They were set to kick off this thing tomorrow. If we really want to put a stop to this it should be as soon as possible. I'm worried that, when they find out what has happened to the warehouse, they will come after us with everything that they have. Not to sound defeatist but if they do kill you two, then Lindsey and I don't stand a chance. We would have to become fugitives forever.'

'Agreed,' said Garrett. 'But I can assure you, prof, it'll take more than this sideshow to kill us two. Lindsey, do your internet thing. See if you can find out any addresses. Let's start with the colonel. He's our biggest threat. Not sure how much longer our luck will last if he keeps sending those SAS boys after us. Then we remove the cop, commander Hastings, he is Haddock's eyes and ears. Without him there's no more access to CCTV for them.

'Finally, Haddock. But we need to do something special there. Also, we have to be very careful, to coin an old cliché; we are sitting on a powder keg here. If we take out these people and the cops start to look for us, then there is no way on God's green earth that we will ever be able to get away or to hide. We will have been responsible for the assassination of three top UK officials.'

'But I can tell them about the whole conspiracy,' interjected Bradley. 'The nuclear weapon, the kidnappings.'

'Oh yes,' agreed Garrett. 'But that would make little to no difference. I know that I sound cynical, but I've done work for these types before. Trust me. This sort of thing simply cannot be allowed to go public. If

the rest of the world discovered that three top UK officials as well as a raft of their underlings were plotting
to detonate a nuclear device on sovereign soil, the shit
would hit the fan in a big way. The United Kingdom
would be vilified. They would become the laughing
stock of the intelligence world. No – they cannot allow
that to happen. If we don't do this properly then we will
all die. So, firstly, I need to put a plan together and,
secondly, we can never talk about this to anyone...ever.
Agreed?'

There were nods all round.

CHAPTER THIRTY-THREE

There were six people at the dinner table. The colonel knew them all. In fact, they were, strictly speaking, his wife's friends, but he had known them for years.

And he still struggled to remember their names. The fat one was called Susan; of that he was fairly sure.

'Darling,' his wife, Penelope, said to him. 'Sally was just telling me that their Tim has been accepted to Edinburgh to read philosophy. Isn't that grand?'

Peterson nodded and smiled his general all-purpose smile, broad enough to show approval but not so broad as to seem false.

'Sally,' he thought to himself. 'The fat one is Sally. Not Susan.'

His wife stood up from the table and went to fetch the main course, the starter having already been cleared away. It had been some sort of grilled white cheese on a bed of rocket, or lamb's lettuce, or some form of salad that had, up until recently, been considered a weed by most normal people.

The main course was sustainable, line caught fish. Poached and served with a side of organic vegetables and couscous.

Peterson hated fish, but it was being served in deference to the fact that one of the guests was a vegetarian. Or pescatarian. Or whatever it was that people called themselves when they wanted to inconvenience the host.

Peterson would have preferred to have a few of his own friends at the table. But for the fact that he had none. He was a career military man and, as such, he had higher ranking officers, officers of equal rank and those below him. Not friends. He had no time for friends.

So instead, he had to break bread with fat people called Sally, and people that eschewed meat.

His wife said something else and he smiled again.

After tomorrow things would be very different.

He'd be the second most powerful person in the country. A man of power and means and influence. He'd probably get rid of Penelope. Push her discreetly to the side. Maybe a small apartment in Sloan Square or thereabouts.

No more conversations about curtains, or swags, or seventy percent wool carpet. (You can't tell the difference, you know. It's just the same as the hundred percent).

No more boring dinners with pretentious women and tofu nibblers.

He smiled to himself.

'Oh look, Dudley,' said one of the women as she held up a bottle of the red wine. 'Two thousand and two. It's older than our youngest son, Tarquin.'

A ripple of polite laughter washed across the table. Ice clicked against crystal water tumblers. The fire crackled and popped in its grate.

Outside a squirrel scuttled up an oak tree, seeking safety in the upper reaches.

At ground level, an urban fox skulked silently away from a darker shadow that moved stealthily past.

A sound of steel defiling human flesh.

A slow exhalation of breath. Of life leaving the body. Escaping its earthly bounds.

Petrus stepped over the prostate guard, moving on to check for any more before gesturing to Garrett to follow.

'I'll take the bodies to the car,' whispered Petrus. 'We can dispose of them later. You go and do your thing.'

Garrett slid forward, heading for the house.

'Look, I don't mind the Poles,' said one of the men around the dinner table. 'Good builders, hard workers and, let's not forget, their women are gorgeous. But it's these other fellows. Mainly from Africa. Asylum seekers, my lily-white ass. More like free housing, schools and medical seekers if you ask me.'

'I agree,' said Peterson's wife. 'And it's not that they're of color. I mean, some of my best friends are of color. Well, acquaintances at the very least. Close acquaintances. It's the way that they act, killing and raping and stealing. It's not right.'

A sash window slid upwards on silent runners.

Then a shade flitted through the house, peering through doors. Pausing to listen and then moving on.

'And as for the benefit classes,' continued Penelope. 'You know, we should be spending more money on defense, bobbies on the beat, grammar schools. Instead, we spend billions on illegal immigrants and foreign aid.'

Peterson leaned back in his chair, his face a picture of smug superiority. All knowing. A man of significance.

Whilst the lesser people amongst us complain, he thought. The giants amongst us do.

'Darling', called Penelope. 'Be a sweetheart and go down to the cellar and fetch up another bottle of the red, would you?'

The colonel stood up, and bowed theatrically. 'Your wish is my command,' he said as he left the room, heading for the cellar.

Down the plush carpeted corridor, left into the kitchen, down the stairs at the back.

He flicked the light switch. Three shelves of wine racks. Mainly full.

He picked up a bottle of red.

The door clicked closed behind him.

He turned.

'Good evening colonel.' A voice in the shadows.

The bottle slipped from nerveless fingers. Shattering on the floor.

'Who are you?'

Garrett stepped forward into the light.

'I am one of the men you and your boys have been trying to kill. Rather unsuccessfully, I might add.'

'Why are you here?'

'I am here to witness your death,' answered Garrett.

'I don't understand. What do you mean?'

Garrett drew the silenced, olive green, military issue Walther P99 from his belt.

Colonel Peterson shrank back.

'Don't worry, colonel,' said Garrett. 'I'm not going to shoot you.'

'Not?' questioned the colonel.

Garrett shook his head and then reversed his hold on the pistol handing it over to Peterson, butt first.

The colonel took it hesitantly.

With one swift movement Garrett moved forward and twisted the colonel's arm, forcing the barrel of the Walther up against his temple.

'No,' said Garrett. 'You are going to shoot yourself.'

The pistol cracked.

Blood sprayed across the room, speckling the bottles and the walls.

Garrett let the man drop to the floor, the pistol still clutched in his dead hand.

Then he left the house on silent feet.

A minute later the fox also slunk away, confident that the coast was clear.

CHAPTER THIRTY-FOUR

Commander Jarvis Hastings was a cliché. Divorced, a functioning alcoholic, clinically depressed and a slave to his career. To get anywhere in the police force wasn't an easy task and it pretty much necessitated a mindset that lived to work as opposed to working to live.

His children came a poor second, and marriage an even more destitute third.

But he had risen to one of the most powerful positions in London and, very soon, he would be in one of the most powerful positions in the country.

He lived in a small one-bedroom apartment on the slightly less fashionable side of the river. Battersea Park. A view of the Thames. A small balcony. Open plan living area. Ikea.

It was on the forty fifth floor. Two below the penthouse. The view and the balcony made up for the diminutive proportions.

His wife had kept the house in Wimbledon, and the two children, Charles and Sophie, were at a good private school, courtesy of his wife's parents.

'I'll be going then, commander,' said the woman standing behind him.

Jarvis waved her away without looking up. 'Fine, Marcy. The guard will let you out.'

She hesitated a few seconds and then turned and left via the front door.

Jarvis had long ago started using prostitutes to relieve, if not his loneliness, at least his physical frustrations. He only used top quality girls and he never paid. There were some advantages to being the commander of the London City Police.

He stood up and pulled his white bathrobe tighter around him, retying the belt as he did so.

Then he built himself a drink. Scotch, a splash of soda and a generous helping of ice. He took a sip and then added more Scotch, filling the tumbler to the brim.

He selected a cigarette from his tabletop silver cigarette box. They were one of his few indulgences. Handmade Turkish cocktail cigarettes. A strong blend wrapped in various different colored papers. Heady and full of flavor. His wife had hated them.

Despite Haddock's warnings about their safety, Hastings felt very safe and secure.

After all, he was on the top of a tall building. There was limited access to the block and only one door. A door that was steel reinforced and protected by a guard. There was another guard in the lobby and yet another patrolling the exterior of the building.

He had nothing to worry about.

The commander lit his cigarette and walked out onto his balcony to look at the view.

It was freezing cold but he never let that deter him. He loved standing out, five hundred feet above the hurly burly of the city, the view stretching across the river and on, taking in the thousands of houses and apartments and office blocks all the way to the horizon.

Something twitched at the corner of his vision and he turned to look.

It took him a few seconds to comprehend what he was actually looking at before a wave of fear washed over him.

It was a rope.

Hanging down from the top of the building and terminating at his balcony.

'Good evening, commander,' greeted Garrett.

Hasting swung around and noticed, for the first time, a man standing in the shadow almost right next to him.

The man smiled. And it was the most terrifying thing that the policeman had ever seen.

'Time to pay the piper, Jarvis,' the man said.

Then he slammed the commander in the chest with the heel of his hand, smashing him backwards over the railing.

And sending him plummeting to earth.

Amazingly he never screamed. Nor did he drop his tumbler of whisky until he hit the ground.

A shadow flitted upwards from the balcony, like a puff of black smoke from a funeral pyre.

CHAPTER THIRTY-FIVE

A s was her habit, Debra woke early. Five thirty. She splashed cold water on her face, tied her hair back, donned a tracksuit and then spent the next forty minutes on her exercise bike, keeping her pulse rate at optimum for the required thirty minutes.

Afterwards she showered, made her face up. Clarins and Estee Lauder. Subtle. Hair, sleek and businesslike.

A light spray of Joy eau de parfum.

She could hear the soft voice of sergeant Robhurst as he talked to one of the other bodyguards in her kitchen, as they helped themselves to coffee. She knew that two other SAS guards were outside. One in the front of the gabled Georgian house and one in the garden at the back.

The house was situated in Barnes, a stone's throw from the river. Two bedrooms and a dressing room upstairs. Eat in kitchen, sitting room and study on the ground floor.

Nett value around the one-million-pound mark. And Debra owned it outright.

She lived alone. Completely single. No boyfriend. And, contrary to some theories, no girlfriend either.

Utterly dedicated to power in all of its forms. Control. Command.

She glanced at her watch, seven o'clock. Time to phone colonel Peterson.

The phone rang for a while before it was answered. 'Yes?'

'Colonel?'

'No ma'am. This is detective inspector Regis. To whom am I speaking?'

'Councilor Haddock. Listen DI, put me through to the colonel.'

'Sorry, ma'am, can't do.'

'Why?'

'Unfortunately, I have to inform you that the colonel is deceased, ma'am.'

There was a long pause while Haddock processed the information. Finally, she spoke again. 'What do you mean, deceased? As in dead?'

'It's the only version of deceased that I know of, ma'am. Died last night. The official verdict's not out yet but it's almost definitely suicide. Shot himself with an SAS issue pistol. Did it in the wine cellar, while his guests were upstairs at a dinner party. No chance of foul play. The doors were locked and there were plenty of witnesses saying that no one else was there.'

'What about his guards?' asked Haddock.

'There were no guards, ma'am.'

'Of course there were, DI. Two of them. SAS.'

'Sorry, ma'am. No guards.'

Debra disconnected the call.

Her hand shook as she scrolled through her address book looking for another number.

Commander Jarvis Hastings.

Dialed. It rang until it cut off. No messages. Nothing.

She tried again. The same result.

Again, she scrolled through her numbers. Looking for commander Hastings' office number.

The duty sergeant answered.

'Commander Hastings please. It's Councilor Haddock. Urgent.'

'I'm sorry, missus Haddock,' replied the desk sergeant. 'But I'm afraid that I have some rather dreadful news. Commander Hastings is dead.'

'What?' shrieked Haddock, as she began to lose control.

'I'm so sorry, madam,' continued the sergeant. 'The commander took his own life last night. Jumped from his balcony.'

'No,' shouted Debra. 'That's impossible. He was murdered.'

'Sorry, ma'am. But he was in his apartment, alone. No access to the building, let alone his apartment. Dreadful thing, just dreadful.'

Haddock ended the call and sat down on her bed. The world spun around her, a coracle at sea. Colors seemed muted. Sound came at her from a great distance away, like an approaching locomotive. She couldn't breathe. It was like her throat had closed up, or her tongue had gotten huge. The size of a loaf of bread.

Then she slowly regained her bearings. Battened down her hatches.

'Robhurst,' she screeched as she walked out of her room. 'Get the driver and the men; we've got to get to the warehouse ASAP. Move it.'

The SAS sergeant looked up at her as she stormed into the kitchen and his face registered his shock at her pale and drawn features.

'Jesus, Debra,' he blurted. 'What's wrong?'

'It's missus Haddock, or Councilor, sergeant,' she snapped. 'We need to get to the warehouse. Now.'

Haddock and her entourage piled into their respective cars and took off at speed, heading for the warehouse.

They crawled slowly through the city's morning rush hour traffic. But as they got closer to the industrial complex, they could see the pillar of black smoke rising into the dull morning air, even though the sun had not yet completely risen.

The driver pulled into the industrial complex but a uniformed policeman stopped them some fifty yards from the warehouse. Standing next to the officer was a fireman, his kit stained black with charcoal, his face wet with sweat. He was drinking from a two-liter bottle of water.

Haddock opened her door, stepped out of the car and approached the policeman.

'What's going on here?' she demanded.

'Not sure, ma'am,' answered the policeman. 'But you are required to keep back, for your own safety.'

'You,' Haddock gestured at the fireman, 'Do you have any idea what's going on or are you as ill-informed as this moron here'

'Steady on, ma'am,' warned the policeman.

'Fuck you,' snapped Haddock.

The officer shook his head and decided to simply ignore the woman in an attempt to keep some of his dignity intact.

The fireman took another deep swig of his water before he spoke. 'Explosions reported last night, emergency services rushed there. No idea what caused it. The warehouse has been totaled. Not a wall left standing.'

Haddock stood dead still for almost ten seconds, her eyes wide, mouth slightly open, face pale.

'No,' she shouted. 'Put it out.' She pushed the fireman in the chest. 'Go and do your job,' she shrieked. 'Stop standing around and do something.'

The fireman took a step back. 'Hey,' he retorted. 'Settle down, you mad bitch.'

'I'll mad bitch you, you fuck head,' squealed Debra. 'Do you know who I am?'

'I don't give a shit,' answered the fireman. 'Just calm down.'

Haddock pushed the man again but, before he could react, sergeant Robhurst grabbed Debra from behind;

wrapping his arms around her, picking her up and carrying her to the car. He opened the back door and bundled her in, instructing the driver to get going as he did so.

'Get your hands off me, you gorilla,' shouted Haddock.

Robhurst grabbed her by her shoulders and shook her. 'Shut up, you moron,' he said. 'Suck it up, pull yourself together. You're losing it. What's wrong with you?'

Haddock stared at the sergeant blankly for a moment and then she started to cry. Great heaving, wet sobs. 'It's all over,' she howled. 'Years of work. Gone. The commander is dead. The colonel is dead. The warehouse is gone. A whole lifetime of labor and nothing to show for it.' She took another shuddering breath, her nose ran down her face and her cheeks glistened with oily tears, glowing bright red under her makeup.

Robhurst pulled out a hanky and thrust it at her. 'Jesus Christ, wipe your face.'

Haddock scrubbed her face with the hanky, wiping off the snot and tears.

'Now you listen,' continued sergeant Robhurst. 'You carry on acting the ass like this and you'll lose a lot more. Treason, murder, sedition. They will send us to a place that makes Guantanamo look like a children's fucking birthday party. So just buck up. Now.'

Haddock took a deep breath. 'You're right. You're right. Thank you, sergeant. So, what do we do now?'

'How the fuck should I know? Nothing, would be my best bet.'

'But what if they come for us?'

'Oh, they will,' assured Robhurst. 'Of that we can be sure. It's just a question of when.'

'Can we stop them?' questioned Debra.

Robhurst shrugged. 'I'm still alive and I've had all sorts trying to change that. I reckon we've got a chance. Anyway, I'm not going to simply sit back and wait for them like a lamb to the slaughter. I know people. I've got favors owed. And as we all know; the best form of defense is a good offence.'

'We still don't even know who they are,' pointed out Debra.

'It really doesn't matter,' observed the sergeant. 'They want us dead; we don't want to be dead. That's all the knowledge that we need.'

They drove home.

Debra sniveled quietly; her face turned away from the SAS sergeant as she did so.

CHAPTER THIRTY-SIX

That morning they moved from the budget hotel of the night before and gone up market. Two adjoining suites in the Soho Hotel, a boutique hotel in the middle of Soho, London - complete with all luxuries and mod cons.

Garrett, Petrus, Lindsey and Bradley were all sitting in Bradley's hotel room drinking room service tea and talking.

'When do we sort out the fish lady?' asked Petrus.

'Fish Lady?'

'Haddock.'

Garrett grinned. 'Not yet. We've stopped her ears and blinded her eyes. We've also drawn her teeth, so there's nothing to fear there.'

'So, what do we do next?'

'We let her stew for a while.'

'Bouillabaisse,' laughed Lindsey, referring to the famous French fish stew.

'Okay, enough fish jokes,' said Garrett. 'It's starting to get painful. Petrus, you came here for a holiday, we're in London so, for the next few days let's do some tourist stuff.'

'Cool,' responded Petrus. 'I'm in.'

Garrett turned to Lindsey. 'You fancy being a tourist guide?'

She nodded.

'What about you, Bradley?' continued Garrett. 'You keen to wander around London with us?'

The prof shook his head. 'I'm working on something here. Need a bit more time. You lot go ahead.' The professor was sitting at the table. On it were arrayed a selection of tools and instruments. No one bothered asking exactly what he was doing because his answers were usually beyond understanding anyway. Garrett knew that he would tell them all when he was ready to.

'I want to buy a jacket,' said Petrus.

'I'll take you to Oxford Street,' suggested Lindsey.

'Whatever. A nice jacket. Tweed. Proper English.'

'Tweed is so lame,' countered Lindsey.

'Tweed,' repeated Petrus, his mind made up.

Garrett smiled as they all left the room and headed for the elevators, happy that, for now, the killing was over and his friend could actually have a little bit of a holiday.

As they rode down to the ground floor, Lindsey's agile mind was already working on an itinerary.

'First we're going to go full tourist,' she said. 'Tower of London, open top bus ride, Madam Tussard's, the London Eye. Then we'll take in a couple of restaurants and sights. If you guys want to go drinking or whatever you'll have to do it at night on your own. I can go into some pubs with you, but really only to eat.'

'Hey, slow down,' grinned Petrus. 'First my jacket, then we're at your mercy.'

'Tweed,' sniffed Lindsey as the doors opened. 'Really.'

Many men who retired from the SAS went on to easier higher paid work in the private security world. Protecting spoilt movie stars, paranoid 'dot com' kids and self captains of industry.

Some set their sights lower and went into the same business but with less salubrious company, but even higher wages.

A favorite category of employer in London being the new bevy of oligarchs and international conmen that Russia was exporting into the rest of Europe. Amongst these men, and women, an ex-SAS servant was a sign of prestige. A mark of one's success.

And once a member of 'The Regiment' always a member.

After sergeant Robhurst had arrived back at Debra Haddock's house he had got straight onto the phone, tracking down various past members of The Regiment, ostensibly those working for Russian hard men. Russian men with both power and influence.

These were the men who ran many of London's clubs, casinos, whore houses and drug dens. Men with plenty of eyes and ears on the street.

They were also men who dealt in a commodity that Robhurst could afford, namely – favors. They would happily do him a favor as long as it was accepted that he, in turn, would be called upon to return the compliment with an equal, or probably bigger, measure. An assassination of a rival, the threatening of a law enforcement officer or the simple beating of someone who had gotten out of line.

After three straight hours on the cell, Robhurst had traded five favors for an army of eyes and ears on the street.

Now over four hundred doormen, bouncers, minicab drivers, prostitutes, croupiers, drug dealers and their clientele would be looking for men of Garrett and Petrus' description. As well as the girl and her father. It wouldn't be long and Robhurst would know where they were.

Then Robhurst went to Haddock and told her of his plan. She wasn't that happy to learn that she would be left alone when the sergeant went out to hunt down their enemy but, as Robhurst explained, it didn't matter because he was certain of exterminating them. So her safety was guaranteed.

CHAPTER THIRTY-EIGHT

Petrus stepped out of the cab, holding the door open for Lindsey. Garrett followed, pausing at the passenger window to pay the driver.

The Zulu, adjusted the collar of his new jacket. An Edgar black and gray basket weave, heavyweight cashmere tweed, based on the jackets worn by Edgar Allan Poe. It fit perfectly, showing off his wide shoulders and narrow hips, the large bellows pockets on the side, perfect for storing spare magazines or hip flasks of whisky.

Even Lindsey had admitted that the coat was 'well cool' when Petrus had tried it on.

After the coat buying exercise, the three of them had gone on a lightning tour of London's tourist spots, taking in The Tower and The London eye, a huge Ferris wheel next to the Thames that gave one a real bird's eye view of the magnificent old metropolis.

Petrus had been impressed by the city and the black cabs, but less so with the outrageous prices of everything. Particularly working with the weak South African Rand, a currency that was almost twenty to one against the Pound. Even a short cab trip cost more than the average week's salary back at home. Fortunately, Garrett covered most of the costs from his seemingly inexhaustible supply of ready cash.

The doorman opened the front door to the Soho hotel, and the three walked into the lobby. The entrance area was dominated by a massive statue of a black cat, the rest of the area an eclectic mix of traditional and ultra-modern British.

They took the elevator to their rooms on the fourth floor. The doors opened into a long corridor, turquoise walls and dark gray carpet, bright blue wooden benches down the side along the walls.

As they stepped out, Lindsey turned to Petrus to make a comment on the outrageous colors when the air around then was torn apart with the whip and crack of passing shot.

Three men stood in the corridor; all were firing at them with semi-automatic pistols.

Petrus threw himself in front Lindsey, knocking her to the floor. But he was too late. A puff of red mist flew into the air as the 9mm bullet struck her, spinning her body as she fell.

Lead ricocheted off the walls and splintered the mirror in the elevator.

Garrett drew his Walther and ran forward, firing as fast as he could.

Petrus jumped up next to him, also drawing and firing as he ran. At the same time the Zulu was screaming incoherently.

The door to their rooms opened and Bradley stepped out.

One if the attackers turned to fire at the professor but Garrett double tapped him as he turned, striking him in the neck and shoulder.

Bradley ducked back into the room.

Petrus ran out of ammo and dropped his pistol to draw his assegai. As he did so the second hit man fired, striking the Zulu in his left bicep, the steel jacketed bullet punching through the muscle and hitting the wall behind him.

And then Petrus was on him, ramming the wide blade of the assegai into the man's eye and smashing him backwards into the wall, then withdrawing the blade and savagely slicing his throat open.

The third assassin turned and ran, leaving via the fire exit at the end of the corridor.

Both Garrett and Petrus turned and sprinted back to Lindsey. She lay on the floor, a pool of blood on her one side.

Petrus turned her over.

The bullet had struck her high on her left deltoid, grazing her deeply but at least the wound was far from lethal. Lindsey whimpered quietly, her whole body shivering with shock.

'Go and kill that animal that ran away,' said Petrus. 'I'll take care of this.'

'I'm on it,' said Garrett. 'You make sure you get out of here ASAP. I'll see you at the first hotel that we stayed in at Earl's Court. Move it, don't forget Bradley. If Lindsey needs a hospital take her to one, her safety exceeds all other needs.'

'Go,' shouted Petrus.

Garrett spun on his heel and sprinted back down the corridor, banging through the fire door. He paused as he got outside, cocking his head to one side as he listened.

Footsteps.

Running.

He looked up.

On the roof.

The assassin had gone up. It was a good move; if Garrett hadn't stopped to listen, he would have naturally assumed that the man would head for the street and he would have gone down in pursuit, losing any chance of catching him.

He raced up the fire escape, taking three steps at a time, his Walther in his right hand.

When he got to the top, he threw himself over the ledge onto the roof, rolling as he did so. A bullet sang off the steel stairway behind him and Garrett kept rolling until he was sheltered behind an air-conditioning unit. Then he dropped to his belly and wriggled forward, poking his head around the bottom of the steel unit. He caught a glimpse of his target, running towards the edge of the roof and then jumping, crossing from the hotel onto the roof of the next building.

Garrett sprang up and ran after him, pausing momentarily before he jumped to the next building, a seven-foot chasm ten stories high. He hit the roof and rolled again, thumping up against the elevator housing. He stood up and scanned the area.

The assassin wasn't there. Garrett ran around the rooftop, checking out the surrounding buildings before spotting his assailant leaping from the next-door roof onto a balcony in the adjacent building.

Garrett followed, grunting with the effort as he drove himself to his top speed, throwing caution to the wind.

He hit the balcony and followed the man up the attached fire escape onto the roof. All around neon lights flashed and hummed. Steam vents opened out onto the rooftops, expelling fragrant steam from restaurant kitchens and release valves on heating systems.

The pink and red and purple neon lights lit up the steam in a haze of hellish color.

Hieronymus Bosch – Christ's Descent into Hell.

Another rooftop. Another jump. Garrett landed badly, slipping in a torrent of water that sluiced across the roof from a broken water pipe. The River Styx.

A shot rang out and a ricocheted off the wall, missing Garrett by mere inches. Then he heard the target running down the fire escape. Boots ringing out on the steel staircase. He followed, running fast. Jumped.

He hit the ground only ten yards or so behind the target who was dodging through the people on the crowded street. Then the assassin took an abrupt left turn, into a narrow alley way. Garrett pounded in behind him.

There were no street lights and the alley smelled strongly of kitchen refuse. Rotten vegetables, fried food and cleaning products. No people. There was one doorway the end of the alley, obviously leading into a restaurant kitchen

The man ran to the end of the alleyway and grabbed the handles and yanked hard.

The door was locked.

He reacted instantly, spinning and firing at Garrett. Three shots and then his slide wracked back on an empty magazine. He threw the weapon at Garrett, obviously completely out of ammunition, and he drew a knife. A Ka-Bar Big Brother. Fifteen inches of serrated, blackened steel.

In turn, Garrett holstered his Walther and drew his Machete.

He stopped some ten feet from the man.

They stood and stared at each other for a few seconds before the man spoke.

'Who the fuck are you guys?'

'I could ask the same of you,' retorted Garrett.

'I'm sergeant Robhurst. Seconded to The Regiment. I'm the guy who is going to kick your ass.'

The Beast growled as it came to the fore. 'Robhurst. The child killer,' it grunted. 'The remover of little girl's fingers.'

The sergeant took a step back, visibly shocked at the change that had come over the man in front of him. From cold eyed combatant to wild eyed animal. He could see that the man was barely under control, his whole body vibrating with energy. With anger. A primal rage.

The Beast attacked.

Robhurst parried and danced, bringing his years of training, of experience and natural ability into play.

But it was to no avail.

He was as a sapling in a tempest.

A fox against a wolf.

Sparks flew as the steel blades clashed together, moving faster than the average human eye could perceive. Circles of flashing steel in the night.

Windmills of death.

And then Garrett struck.

With an almost casual blow he struck Robhurst on the left wrist. The sergeant's hand leapt from his arm, followed by a jet of blood. He dropped his blade and fell to the floor, clutching his wrist tightly in an attempt to staunch the flow of blood.

'Why did you do it?' asked Garrett. 'How could you kill a little girl?'

Robhurst looked up at him and sneered. 'What is one girl's life compared to the wellbeing of an entire country? The few suffer so that the many may prosper.'

Garrett shook his head 'It doesn't work like that.'

Robhurst laughed, his voice harsh with pain and shock. 'Yes, it does. Grow up.'

'Well, it shouldn't,' said Garrett, his voice low. 'It's wrong.'

'Fuck you,' cursed Robhurst.

Garrett shook his head. 'No. Fuck you.'

The machete struck again and the sergeant's headless corpse fell to the floor.

CHAPTER THIRTY-NINE

Garrett arrived at the hotel in Earl's Court just before midnight. He had left the area using the rooftops to get as far as he could before returning to street level, hoping that he would have avoided any CCTV cameras as they weren't positioned on the tops of the buildings.

Then he had walked to Earl's Court and the hotel so that there was no record of him either on public transport or using a black cab.

He knocked on the door. Petrus answered and let him in, pistol in hand.

'How is Lindsey,' asked Garrett as the door closed.

'She's okay,' replied Petrus. I bandaged her arm up and organized a course of broad-spectrum antibiotics and a handful of codeine. I had to bribe the pharmacist a hundred pounds to obtain the drugs without a prescription, but that wasn't a problem. She's taken a few Codeine, so she's as high as a kite.'

Garrett went through the adjoining door into the next room. Bradley was sitting at the table and Lindsey was perched on the end of her bed.

She looked at Garrett and then she pointed her finger and cocked her thumb at him, like a pistol. 'Bang!' she giggled. 'I got shot. Fuck me.'

'Language,' retorted Garrett halfheartedly, too pleased to see the girl relatively unharmed to actually be angry at her swearing.

'Yeah,' she agreed. 'Got shot.'

Her head fell forward and she slipped slowly onto her side. Asleep.

Petrus rushed over, pulled her to her pillows and covered her with a blanket.

'She'll be fine,' he said.

Bradley walked over to the bed and sat next to his daughter, stroking the hair from her closed eyes and then holding her hand as she slept.

'So,' continued Petrus. 'You took care of the last guy?'

'Yep. He was the child murderer.'

'Bastard. Also,' Petrus picked up his jacket. 'The animal ruined my jacket.' He stuck his finger through a large bloody hole in the left sleeve.

Garrett chuckled. 'How is your arm?'

'Hurts like hell,' answered Petrus. 'Combine that with the hole in my forearm and we can write off my hand-to-hand combat skills for a while. I suppose that I could take some happy pills but they'll take the edge off my alertness. Maybe later. Anyhow, what now?'

'We need to get Haddock before she runs. If she goes to ground, we might never find her.'

Bradley stood up from the bed and took Lindsey's cell phone out. 'Here,' he said, pointing at some writing on the screen. 'I tracked down her address.'

'I'll go there now,' said Garrett.

Petrus stood up. 'I'll go with you.'

'Why, so that you can wave at any attackers? Shoo them away with vigorous hand movements?' asked Garrett sarcastically.

'Piss off,' laughed Petrus. 'I can still shoot.'

'True, let's go.'

'Wait,' interjected Bradley. 'I have something to show you. This may sound…odd, but please just listen before you pass comment.'

Both Garrett and Petrus turned to look at the professor.

Okay,' said Garrett. 'Talk to us.'

The professor held up a small white container of pills. 'I want you to take these with you.'

And then he explained why.

CHAPTER FORTY

It was about two o'clock in the afternoon when Garrett parked the Land Rover down the street from the address the prof had given them.

'I'm going in through the back,' he told Petrus. 'You stay out front. Keep guard. Don't take any chances. You see someone coming in the front door who looks like trouble then just shoot them.'

The Zulu nodded. 'Will do.'

Garrett checked his pocket for the small box the professor had given him, then he stepped out of the Land Rover and walked down the street until he was next to the house.

First, he checked for pedestrians and then, seeing none, jumped the fence, into Haddock's back yard.

The yard was small and well maintained. A water feature, small pond with Koi Carp. A set of garden furniture with two seats.

Roses and shrubs filled the beds, but they had all been pruned back for the winter. Spare dry sticks, pointing upwards into the slate gray sky like a graveyard of dead men's fingers.

Garrett ghosted over to the back door that entranced into the kitchen. His pistol was still in his belt and his machete in its shoulder holster. He waited and listened.

He could hear someone inside. One person walking around. Probably in the sitting room that appeared to be situated off the kitchen.

He tested the door handle.

Locked.

He stood back, raised his foot to his chest and slammed it into the lock. The door literally exploded into the room, tearing off its hinges and bouncing off the kitchen table onto the floor.

Garrett ran in after it, sprinting through the kitchen and into the sitting room.

Haddock stood there, her face a mask of utter shock and surprise.

Garrett stepped up to her and punched her in the face.

She went down, hit the floor and lay there, shaking her head, blood pouring from her nose.

'Are you alone?' asked Garrett.

She looked up at him, her face still drawn in shock and pain.

He nudged her with his foot. 'Are you alone?' he repeated.

She nodded.

Garrett grabbed her and pulled her to her feet where she swayed from side to side like a drunken sailor. He cast his gaze about the house and then dragged her across the room and into the study where he sat her roughly down on one of the office chairs next to the desk.

'I assume you have killed sergeant Robhurst,' she stated, her voice rough with pain and fear.

'Yes, and his two accomplices.'

Haddock closed her eyes for a second. 'Who are you?'

'I'm one of the men who you've been trying to kill.'

'Yes,' she nodded slightly. 'I worked that out. But who are you? Who do you work for? CIA? MI6?'

'No one,' answered Garrett. 'I'm simply the spanner in the works. The ghost in the machine. I suppose you could say, I am the living proof that karma happens.'

'I don't understand.'

Garrett sneered at the politician. 'Your understanding is utterly irrelevant. However, there are a few things that I would like to know. Merely for my own enlightenment.'

'Are you going to kill me?' asked Haddock.

'I think that I will ask the questions,' countered Garrett. He stared at her for a while, then he spoke again. 'Why?' he asked. 'That's what I want to know. Why were you going to do it?'

Debra smiled. 'If you have to ask then you will never understand the answer.'

'Try me,' countered Garrett.

'I was trying to save our country. Our way of life. Our world.

'We are at war, but our leaders are too shit scared to admit it. They waffle on about proportional response and multiculturalism. They don't even have the balls to name their enemy. Islam. Those Koran reading fanatical mass murderers are eating away at the very fabric of our society.

'They have reviled us as the enemy and they have declared war, while we still wave pieces of paper around and talk about peace in our time like Will fucking Chamberlin did with the Nazis. England has become a training ground for the very people that have sworn to destroy us and all that our politicians do is work out more ways to accept them into our society. More ways to support them with free housing and education and medical aid so that they can grow up and blow us to kingdom come.'

Garrett shook his head. 'So, your solution was to detonate a nuclear weapon on our own soil, and blame it on the Muslims?

'To kill innocent British people? Thousands would die the most horrific deaths from the radioactive fallout as they contracted radioactive poisoning.

'Severe diarrhea. Vomiting. Debilitating headaches. Liver and kidney failure. Hair and tooth loss.

'Death.

'No cure.

'Women, children, young and old.'

Haddock shrugged. 'Omelet. Eggs. What can I say? To lead one has to be strong.'

'Strong, yes,' admitted Garrett. 'Psychotic, no. You cut a little girl's finger off and then killed her.'

'I didn't do that,' argued Haddock. 'That was Rob-hurst.'

'You ordered him to,' snapped Garrett. And The Beast snarled in the background.

'Oh, Jesus Christ, you sanctimonious prick,' shrieked Haddock. 'Stop being so pathetic. We are at war. Children die. It's called collateral damage. Grow up.'

'No, it's called murder.'

'Fuck you,' yelled Haddock. 'Just shoot me and get it over with.'

Garrett shook his head. 'I'm not going to shoot you,' he said. 'As much as I want to, I made a promise.'

A tiny glimmer of hope flickered across Debra's face. 'What are you going to do?'

Garrett drew out his machete. The steel blade rasped against the leather holster as he slid it out, the kitchen lights picking out the razor-sharp edge.

'No,' gasped Debra. 'Please. Rather shoot me.'

Garrett flicked the weapon up into the air, spinning it and catching it by the flat of the blade. Then he handed it to Haddock.

She stared blankly at it, not moving.

'Take it,' commanded Garrett.

Haddock took a tentative hold of the handle. Garrett let go and the weapon fell to the floor as it slipped from Debra's grasp, much heavier than she expected.

'Pick it up.'

She took hold of it again.

Garrett drew his Walther. 'Now listen carefully,' he said. 'Your life depends upon this. If you do not do as I say, and quickly, then I will shoot you in both knees and then the stomach. You will take hours to die and it will be in absolute agony. Do you understand?'

Debra nodded.

'Good. Now stand up and go to the desk. Sit down in your chair and place your left hand on the table.'

Debra complied, her movements slow and shaky as fear hindered her motor abilities.

'Good,' said Garrett. 'Now take the machete in your right hand and chop off your left hand index finger.'

Haddock did a double take. 'What?'

'You heard,' replied Garrett. 'Do it.'

'No.'

Garrett fired into the table next to Haddock's hand. She jerked backwards in her chair and let out a yelp.

'Do it!' shouted Garrett.

Without thinking Debra brought the machete down. It struck her index finger, cutting deeply but not severing it.

She screamed in agony.

'Again,' commanded Garrett.

She struck again. And again. The third blow separated her digit from her hand as well as cutting deeply into her adjacent ring finger. Blood pooled onto the table, thick and viscous and red. The coppery smell of it filled the room.

Debra dropped the machete and grabbed her wrist, rocking back and forth and keening in agony and shock.

Garrett tucked his Walther into his belt. Then he took a small box from his pocket and opened it. Inside was a field dressing and a container of pills.

He took Haddock's left hand and roughly bandaged the stump of her finger and the cut on her ring finger, pulling the dressing tight enough to stop the bleeding. Then he opened the pill bottle, took two out and placed them in front of Haddock.

'Here,' he said. 'Take these. They're a combination of pain killers and broad-spectrum antibiotics.'

Haddock shook her head.

'Don't be stupid,' insisted Garrett. 'You're not impressing anyone. Just take it, and then take two every day until they're finished.'

Debra grabbed the two capsules and dry swallowed them, staring at Garrett with absolute hatred as she did so.

'What now?' she asked, her voice rough with pain.

'Now,' said Garrett. 'You live with the knowledge of what you are. And every time that you look at your ruined hand, you remember the little girl that you murdered.'

'I still don't understand why you didn't kill me.'

'Because I made a promise to someone,' answered Garrett as he picked up his machete and wiped the blood off the blade with a dishtowel.

Then he rammed it back into its shoulder holster and left the room without looking back.

His work was finished.

He had fulfilled his promise to Professor Bradley.

CHAPTER FORTY-ONE

Petrus sat back in his canvas camping chair and took a sip of his beer.

The sun had just risen over the Valley of a Thousand Hills and he was wearing his new Edgar Tweed jacket. Before he left England, he had insisted on purchasing a new one to replace the bloody one the assassins had ruined.

Truth be told, it was already far too hot to have donned the thick cashmere garment, but he loved it. The quality of the lining, the cut of the material and its superior craftsmanship, all added up to make an item of clothing that was more than simple cloth and stitching. It was a costume. A gentleman's attire.

The cows lowed in the valley as they chewed the cud, their jaws grinding from side to side, their eyes deep pools of solemn contemplation. Above him a Hadeda Ibis flew in concentric circles, looking for insects or snails, its distinctive call echoing across the hills. Ahaa! Ahaa! Ahaa!

Petrus could also hear some of the womenfolk singing down by the river as they collected water and washed clothes, their sweet voices a perfect counterpoint to the bass of the lowing cows and the raucous call of the Ibis.

Home.

A place where the sun rose and fell at a decent hour, and a man could stand bare-chested even during the coldest of the winter months. A place where an hour's parking did not cost a week's salary. A place where the sky was as big and open as a man's dreams.

He flexed his left arm and winced. It had only been four days and his wounds took longer to heal than they used to when he was still in his teens or early twenties.

All said and done, he was sick of being shot. And stabbed.

The Zulu chuckled quietly to himself. Regardless, life was good.

CHAPTER FORTY-TWO

Haddock did not return to parliament the day after Garrett forced her to mutilate herself. Nor the next day. She was utterly exhausted. However, she did not push herself, opting instead to phone in and claim illness.

After all, she reasoned to herself, her life's work had been dashed and she had suffered serious physical trauma. There was no shame in taking some time off, even though the concept was unfamiliar to her.

On the third day she made the decision to go in to London. But she simply could not. She had started to suffer from a serious bout of both nausea and diarrhea, so chronic that she was unable to leave the immediate vicinity of her bathroom.

On the fourth day, the headaches started. Mind blowing pain, the likes of which she had never experienced before. She got out of bed and staggered through to the bathroom, rinsing her mouth and spitting into the washbasin. The water ran deep red. Then she ran her fingers through her hair and great clumps of it came out in her hands.

And she remembered Garrett's statement…

... 'So your solution was to detonate a nuclear weapon on our own soil and blame it on the Muslims? Kill innocent British people? Thousands would die the most horrific deaths from the radioactive fallout as they contracted radioactive poisoning. Severe diarrhea. Vomiting. Debilitating headaches. Liver and kidney failure. Hair and tooth loss. Death. No cure.'

And her flippant reply...

... 'Omelet. Eggs. What can I say? To lead one has to be strong.'

'Polonium poisoning,' she gasped to herself. 'The bastard must have put it in the capsules that he gave me.' Haddock sank slowly to the floor and her eyes filled with tears of self-pity.

She was dying.

In the most horrific way imaginable.

And she knew that there was no cure.

Slowly and painstakingly, she crawled from the bathroom to the kitchen. It took her two attempts to stand and, when she was on her feet, she went straight to the cutlery drawer and took out a small paring knife. A ceramic blade. Japanese. As sharp as a razor.

Then, Debra Haddock, backbencher, councilor of England and rabid patriot, sat down on the kitchen floor and, with one swift movement, cut her left wrist open.

It took her twelve minutes to bleed to death.

CHAPTER FORTY-THREE

Garrett threw the newspaper into the fire and it flared up, filling the room with a bright orange glow.

Debra Haddock's death had been reported as a suicide. The strain of her work. The pressure of being a public servant.

There was no mention of her physical state.

There was no mention of Polonium.

Garrett had known there would not be.

He walked over to his worn old wingback chair and sat down, staring at the flames that twisted and stuttered in the grate. On the table next to him stood a bottle of Laphroig single malt. A powerful, heady whisky well suited to his mood and the lateness of the hour.

He poured a large dram and then held the crystal tumbler up in a toast.

He toasted Daisy. And he toasted Scarlet. Because they were his friends. And because, for them the wars were finally over. They were at peace.

Then he took in a mouthful and swirled it round his mouth, savoring the deep peaty flavor before swallowing.

And he knew that the wars were not over for him. They would never be over.

But, at least for now, the cage had been shut. And bolted.

And The Beast squatted in the corner of its cell and growled quietly at passers by.

Waiting for the next time.

Waiting patiently for its release.

For an excuse.

A reason to kill again.

****

Hi – I hope that you enjoyed this tale. If you would like to have a chat or simply give me some feedback or advice, please email me at *zuffs@sky.com* and I will get straight back to you.

Keep a look out for Garrett and Petrus in their next adventure – A REASON TO KILL.

Thanks again – your friend, Craig.

If you have enjoyed the Garrett & Petrus books so far – why not give my stand-alone novel – The Broken Men, a try?

Here's a short sample…

THE BROKEN MEN

PROLOGUE

*L*eon could hear Peewee clattering around the ho-tel room. An unfamiliar smell of incense permeated the air and he could sense bright light through his closed lids. But try as he might he could not open them. It was as if they had been sewed shut. And the pain from his wounds pulsed through his body in rhythm to his heart. A primal savage cadence, a tribal drum beat. A call to arms. But he could not move. And despair washed over him as he realised that this was probably the end. For him there would be no redemption.

The young Zulu leant over Leon's prostrate body and squeezed his hand in an attempt to get a response. But the hand remained limp. Clammy. Dead. And Leon's call to his friend went unvoiced and unheard. 'Please. Don't let me die. Not now. Not before I have finished. For if not me then who will cleanse the earth of this evil that I helped to create? Who but me can fight this war? I have turned against my people. My country. My friends. I need to finish it.'

And slowly his consciousness slipped away. And as he fell back into darkness, he knew that his young black friend was his only hope. His only hope for atonement. His only way to achieve uBuntu.

And Peewee cast the bones and chanted the magic words and begged his ancestors. For he would do anything, risk everything for this white man. This soldier of darkness that had become his best friend...and his people's greatest hope.

Leon swept the sweat from his face using the back of his hand. They had been running hard for over four hours with full battle packs and the young lieutenant marveled at the fitness of his men. Particularly the machine gunner, a short, wide Zulu that they all called Popeye. His 7.62 mm Mag with eight hundred rounds weighed in at a little over fifty pounds. Together with his food and water this boosted the load to the approximate weight of a ten-year-old male child. Yet he had run alongside Leon for the better part of the morning, never slacking nor complaining.

The land around them shimmered in the harsh African heat. Red sand, copses of scrubby thorn trees and mile after mile of waist high razor-grass. Featureless and barren as an alien world. Even the compasses didn't work due to the high magnetic content of the blood-colored soil.

Leon held his right hand high and swung it around twice, calling his men to him. They jogged up and gathered around. He crooked his finger at the tracker, a tiny *San* bushman on secondment from 31st battalion. The members of Leon's stick referred to him as Tabatha, an approximation of his actual name that was a series of clicks and glottal stops totally unpronounceable by the western tongue.

'Tabatha.'

'Boss man.'

'So, are we getting any closer?'

Tabatha nodded. 'One hour. Maybe less.'

Leon pointed at the sun. 'Show me.'

The bushman described a short arc with his hand. How far the sun would travel in the time that it would take to catch up with their foe. Leon always made the little tracker show him the time because, while he was an almost supernatural hunter, he had no idea of western chronology and so, whenever he was asked a time related question, he would always give the same answer in order to cover his ignorance; 'One hour. Maybe less.'

By showing the arc of the sun he had demonstrated that they were closer to three hours behind the insurgents, not one.

Leon and his team of seven men had been pushing hard since four o'clock that morning. Eating rations on the move, 'dog biscuits' and water. They had been dropped at 'The Cutline' that morning after word was sent down that a group of approximately thirty SWAPO (South West African Peoples Organization) insurgents had crossed the border from Ovamboland into South West Africa.

The night before the insurgents had attacked a farm and killed the family. Mother, father and two daughters. The women and the girls, not yet teenagers, had been repeatedly raped.

'The Cutline' was the animal disease fence that separated the farming communities in South West Africa from Ovamboland and it ran in an eastern direction from Oshivello gate up to Rundu. Some two hundred miles. The group of South African soldiers had tracked the perpetrators back across the line into Ovamboland and were seeking retribution. The enemies four-to-one numerical advantage did not concern them. Not even slightly.

Leon pointed at the spoor and patted Tabatha on the back. 'Let's hunt.'

The bushman grinned widely and took up the spoor, running lightly on his spindle like legs, barefoot and wearing only a skin kirtle and an ostrich shell necklace.

The rest of the stick loped after him, weapons ready. Eyes scanning their surrounds. Constantly alert.

It was Leon's first week at the sharp end, as well as his first command and he was keen to show his worth so he ran his men hard to catch up. Perhaps too hard.

They ran into the ambush at a few minutes before midday. The platinum sun directly overhead cancelled out all shadow and bleached the land into a one-dimensional sepia vista. A lifeless daguerreotype, devoid of movement or colour, which made the sudden eruption of violence all the more shocking.

The Ambush had been well laid, taking advantage of a natural fold in the land that squeezed the hunters closer together. The insurgents had split their group into three sections. Two lined the depression and the third had deployed directly across it.

Fortunately for the South Africans the insurgents sprung the trap prematurely, firing as soon as Tabatha entered the kill zone. The opening fusillade literally tore the tiny bushman apart, picking his child-like body up into the air and hammering it backwards in a spray of blood and flesh.

It was the first time that Leon had actually been in a contact and he froze to the spot as all around him the air came alive with fire. Bullets whipped past him buzzing spitefully as they searched for flesh to rend. His head was nudged to one side by an invisible blow and blood flowed freely down his neck, soaking his battle tunic.

Next to him Popeye returned fire. Long sustained bursts sweeping from side to side. Glittering cartridges cascaded from the Mag as it beat out a frantic rhythm of destruction at a rate of over nine hundred rounds a minute.

And then Leon's training clicked in. *Return fire.* He raised the R1 assault rifle to his shoulder. *Pick your target.* He started firing back at the muzzle flashes that he could see. Aimed double taps. *Move towards the source of attack.* He moved forward, steps steady and unhurried. Momentary flutter of panic as his rifle stopped working. Eject used magazine. Change for fresh. Fire. Fire. *Encourage your troops.*

'Come on, boys. Take them out.'

Leon started to move faster and his troops came with him. Screaming incoherently, firing as they ran. And then they were amongst them. A man appeared out of the grass in front of Leon. He shot him twice. Chest and neck. Another to his left. Bang, bang. Body dropping. Dying legs beating a spastic tattoo on the red soil. An explosion. Grenades. Reload. Kill again. Again.

And then slowly the firing stopped. Wind. The sound of the machine gun barrel pinking sharply as it cooled. High pitched sound of someone in agony. Cut short with a single shot.

Leon pulled in a deep breath. The air felt dead. Stale. Unable to sustain life. His heart hammered in his chest like an animal trying to escape a trap. Someone laughed. No humor. Merely a sound, affirming life.

He slung his rifle over his shoulder. Took out a pack of cigarettes and a Zippo. Put one in his mouth and tried to light with shaking hand. After three attempts he gave up and simply stood, the tube of tobacco sticking out of his lips at a jaunty angle. A child's lollipop stick.

Popeye walked over, took the Zippo from Leon's hand and flicked it to flame. Held the fire under the tip of the cigarette. The young lieutenant drew in. The smoke was harsh. Acrid. Better than the dead air. More alive.

He glanced at the Zulu. 'Thanks. I froze.'

Popeye shook his head. 'No, boss. You done good. We won.'

'We lost Tabatha.'

Popeye shrugged and then pulled a cigarette pack from his webbing. Lit. Inhaled. Gave Leon his Zippo back. 'Not your fault. His fault. Careless. Now dead.'

The stick's sergeant came jogging over with the medic in tow. He threw Leon a casual salute. 'We killed twenty-two, sir. The other eight gapped it. Do you want us to pursue?'

Leon shook his head. 'Did we take any casualties?'

'Only the bushman, sir.'

'Tabatha, sergeant. He has a name.'

'Yes, sir. Of course. Tabatha. I've brought the medic, sir.'

'Why?'

'You've been wounded, sir. Your ear.'

Leon put his hand to the side of his head. Looked at it. Covered in blood. Red. Sticky.

The medic, a Malay of mixed blood from the Cape, stepped forward and checked out Leon's wound. Roughly wiping the blood away with a water-soaked sterile cloth. Then he strapped a bandage to the side of his head, covering the bottom half of his ear.

'That was close, lieutenant. You've lost the bottom bit of your ear. The bleeding should stop soon. How's the pain?'

Leon shook his head.

'Okay, sir. I'll check out the rest of the men, if that's fine by you.'

'Carry on.'

Leon walked slowly across the killing ground. Bodies lay at random intervals. Hardly any lay alone. All had died in groups. Twos, threes and fours. Corpses huddled together. Children hiding from the dark. Some peaceful. Some, faces stretched into grotesques masks of terror held in time by rigor mortis. Others with puzzled expressions. Baffled at the sudden cessation of their short lives.

He saw his ones. His kills. Stopped to look. Forced himself to feel nothing. No remorse. No exaltation. They had been alive. Now they were dead. He had killed them. Three men. The year was nineteen eighty. He was not yet nineteen years old. And only six months before he had finished school and had been on holiday with his friends.

He closed his eyes and remembered…

www.ingramcontent.com/pod-product-compliance
Lightning Source LLC
Chambersburg PA
CBHW061319190726
48288CB00002B/572